THE ASSASSIN'S RESURRECTION

THE ASSASSINS
BOOK 3

MARK ALLEN

ROUGH
EDGES
PRESS

Rough Edges Press
An Imprint of Wolfpack Publishing
1707 E. Diana Street
Tampa, FL 33610

roughedgespress.com

Paperback ISBN 978-1-68549-789-7
eBook ISBN 978-1-68549-399-8
LCCN 2025942231

ALSO BY MARK ALLEN

THE ASSASSIN'S
RESURRECTION

PROLOGUE

GHOSTS GLIDED SILENTLY through the winter night, merciless wraiths obeying the commands of their master, death bristling cold and metallic in their fists as they swarmed the house of their enemy.

The ten-man hit team lacked the polished finesse of trained operators, but they were good enough to get the job done. Guns bucked in gloved fists, bullets chugged from stubby suppressors, and the henchmen who got paid to protect the property of Samuele "Saigon Sammy" Quattro went down like scythed wheat with hearts and heads—sometimes both—blown wide open.

The perimeter patrols went down first, bullets in brainpans. The strike force left them where they fell, leaving red stains in the snow, and moved deeper into the luxurious, five-acre Greystone on Hudson grand estate that served as Quattro's weekend retreat when he wanted to get out of New York City. If they looked over their shoulders and peered through the trees, they might have glimpsed the Tappan Zee Bridge spanning the river in the distance or caught the silver sparkle of moonlight on the water.

But they weren't here to see the sights. They were here to send a message. A lethal warning, written in blood.

The guards stationed just outside the mansion, on the patios and walkways, died next. Their bodies jerked under the impact of suppressor-hushed rounds, followed by *coup de grâce* finishers fired point-blank into eye sockets and nasal cavities. The corpses twitched in death spasms as the departed souls found out dirty money doesn't spend in hell. A hard lesson, learned too late.

They breached the house in a classic pincher attack, blowing open locks with precisely fired bullets, half the men crashing through the back door while the other five assaulters kicked open the front. The guards stationed inside actually managed to put up a fight—perhaps knowing they were the last line of defense made them desperate—and took out two members of the strike team.

But it wasn't enough. A triple-chaser of flash-bangs rendered them blind, ruptured their eardrums, and left them vulnerable. The hitters seized the advantage and sent hot rounds sizzling through enemy flesh.

It was all over in less than a minute. But a lot of dying happened in those sixty seconds.

The strike team leader was a tall, thickly muscled man named Rabideaux, but everyone just called him Rabid for short. He pretended to hate the nickname, but secretly liked it. He felt it suited him because he was a little crazy and sported a mile-wide mean streak.

He'd been appointed head of security after the previous guy had been assassinated, and he took the job very seriously.

He motioned toward the wide, curving staircase that led to the upper floor. Their target—their *prey*— would be barricaded in one of the rooms upstairs, behind a locked door, undoubtedly guarded by his personal protection detail of at least two men, maybe as many as four.

Eight to four odds? Rabid would take it. No way in hell were they leaving here tonight without fulfilling their mission. Their master was cold as an arctic wolf and did not brook failure well.

The hitters swept up the stairs in a ragged two-by-two formation. At the top, a corridor broke off in each direction, one stretching to the right, the other going left. There were multiple doors to choose from, including large double doors at each end of the hall that most likely led to master suites.

Rabid motioned for his guys to peel left. The suite to the right would offer a better view of the river, and he assumed Saigon Sammy would reserve that one for himself. The mob boss wasn't here right now—still vacationing at his home down in the Florida Keys—but Rabid seriously doubted Sammy's son was using his father's bedroom while he was gone.

Which meant Taide Quattro, oldest son of Samuele Quattro and heir to the vast power and wealth of his father's criminal empire, would be holed up in the suite on the left like a shivering rat trapped in a hole watching the wildfire burn toward him.

The eight men lined up on either side of the double

doors. They couldn't hear anything inside the suite, but Rabid knew their quarry was in there. He could feel it, his gut telling him that the hunt was almost over. They just needed to breach and kill, and then they could all go home to cold beer and warm women.

Still, he'd give his enemies a chance to surrender first. If they were willing to give up without a fight, it would mean less risk to his men. He doubted Taide and his bodyguards would comply, but it never hurt to ask.

"Hey, Quattro!" Rabid called out. "Can you hear me in there? Sound off, you piece of shit."

"Sammy's not here!" Someone on the other side of the door shouted the reply.

Beneath his black balaclava, Rabid's lips curved into a knowing smile. What a bunch of worthless meatheads. These amateurs had just confirmed their presence. His gut had not steered him wrong.

"We're not here for Sammy," he replied. "We just want his boy."

"Too fucking bad, asshole. You can't have him."

Rabid's smile sharpened. Now they had confirmed that Taide Quattro was inside.

"Listen," he said. "You got a name?"

"Yeah, first name Fuck, last name You."

"Catchy." Rabid paused for two heartbeats. "All right, cocksucker, here's how this is gonna play out. There're eight of us, and how many of you? Two, three, maybe four? Which means when we come through that door, you're gonna get blitzed about as fast as it takes to slap your momma's ass."

No response from inside the suite.

"But I'll give you a chance to keep on sucking God's

good air," Rabid continued. "Toss your weapons, come out with your hands up, leave Quattro to face the music alone, and you guys can live to die another day."

"Not happening," came the response from the other side of the doors.

Rabid shrugged. It was pretty much the answer he had expected, but it hadn't hurt to take a shot at a peaceful resolution. But now it was time to take shots of a different kind. A *lethal* kind.

"Your fucking funeral, buddy," he muttered, motioning for the hit team to breach the door and get this shit over with.

Bullets quickly chewed open the locks. They cracked the doors just enough to toss in a couple of flash-bangs and stormed inside while Taide's security detail reeled from the blinding, concussive effects of the double detonations. A lucky blind shot from one of the guards put another member of the strike team on the floor with the bridge of his nose bisected by a slug. Losing men pissed Rabid off, but snagging Taide Quattro inside his heavily protected home without suffering any casualties would have been a damned miracle. Losses had been expected, and so far, they were acceptable, if still infuriating.

Turned out there were three men paid to defend Taide Quattro with their lives, and that's exactly what they did. Outnumbered and disoriented from the flash-bangs, the trio of bodyguards never stood a chance. They died on their feet, jerking and thrashing spastically as rounds riddled their bodies before hitting the floor in bloody heaps.

Rabid ignored the carnage and fixed his eyes on the

man still standing. Taide Quattro had a gold-plated Desert Eagle .357 Magnum in his hand, but seemed to have no interest in using it. The semi-automatic blaster hung down at his side, muzzle pointed at the hardwood floor. He stared at the invaders with fear in his eyes.

"Who are you?" he asked, his voice little more than a scared croak. "What do you want?"

Rabid stalked over to him. He despised weakness. Taide Quattro had been born with the proverbial spoon in his mouth, and it showed. Everything about him radiated softness, and his currently quivering chin did nothing to dispel that first impression. Saigon Sammy Quattro was a legitimate badass, a self-made man who had clawed his way to the top through decades of balls and brawn. But his son? Softer than a fuzzy pink slipper full of puppy shit. Rabid wondered if Taide's younger brothers were any better or if the whole damn family was a bunch of pussies.

Rabid reached over and took the Desert Eagle away from him. Taide didn't even try to put up a fight, just relinquished it like a little kid turning over a toy he no longer wanted to play with.

"Who I am is irrelevant," Rabid replied. "What I want...well, what I *want* is to send a message to your father to keep his Soviet sons of bitches off our turf."

"I don't know what you're talking about." Taide looked like he was about to puke.

"I know you don't," Rabid replied. "But your dad does, and the message is for him."

"My phone's in my pocket. You...you want me to, uh, send him, like, a, uh, text or something?"

"No, we'll take care of the texting. We just need you to die first."

Rabid raised the Desert Eagle .357 Magnum.

"No, please!" It was practically a sob, and Taide put a hand up in front of the muzzle as if it would stop the bullet.

It didn't.

The hollow-point punched through his palm like a high-powered crucifixion nail and then hammered him right in the mouth. Blood, brains, and bone shards exploded from the exit wound in the back of his skull.

With all systems violently severed, the corpse barely even twitched when it crashed to the floor. A few little spasms, a little drumming of the heels against the teak boards, and it was over.

Rabid kneeled down beside the corpse, pulled out a knife, and got to work.

————

Samuele "Saigon Sammy" Quattro bolted upright in bed with cold sweat popping out of his pores and soaking the sheets. The scream trapped in his throat died stillborn as he managed to strangle it back, choking on the cry so as to not wake up the young, tanned, and remarkably flexible beach bunny currently slumbering on the far edge of the king-sized bed. Her arm dangled over the side as if she were a corpse.

He couldn't even remember her name, but it didn't matter. Come morning, he would have his private chef shovel some breakfast down her throat and then kick her to the curb. Down here in Key West, golden-skinned beach bunnies willing to ditch their bikinis were a dime a dozen for wealthy and powerful men like himself.

The nightmare receded swiftly, vanishing like cold mist in the hot sun, gone so quickly that all he remembered were fragmented images. Steaming jungle. Torrential rain. Bamboo cages. Sucking mud. Rotting corpses. Maggot-infested flesh.

The POW camp, hell on earth, was his home for nearly a year, for most of '67 and part of '68.

He'd finally managed to escape, taking with him the savage scars both physical and mental. He'd flung his tortured, infected, malnourished body through the unforgiving jungle and never looked back, and even then, he had known that his sleep would forever be haunted by nightmares.

Back then, there had been no fancy names for the soul-trauma, no PTSD hotlines you could dial when the demons came calling in the dead of night. Suck it up and live with it was the name of the game and that's exactly what Saigon Sammy had learned how to do.

He earned his nickname by taking over the heroin-trafficking operation in Saigon. Following his escape from the POW camp, he vowed never to return to the Army that had clearly abandoned him and left him to rot in that putrid, stinking hellhole. He figured they had no idea he had escaped—wasn't like the VC were going to tell them—so there was no reason for him to go back.

He made his way to Saigon, started killing off the heroin dealers, and took over their networks. Not the smartest plan, but it worked, and besides, in his youth, Sammy had always boasted more balls than brains.

Too bad those genetics had not been passed on to his son. Taide, the damn kid, had plenty of smarts but was a real cry-ass. How the hell that boy was ever going to take over the family business, Sammy had no idea.

Maybe he should throw tradition to the wind and consider leaving the reins to one of Taide's younger brothers instead.

As the war ended, he fled Saigon and returned to the States, and quickly made a name for himself in the burgeoning New York City organized crime business. He had street smarts from years of prowling Saigon's back alleys, coupled with a killer's ruthlessness, and the powers that be paid attention. By the time the eighties rolled around, he was king of his own cutthroat empire, running rackets, moving so much coke he damn near needed a snowplow, hustling hookers, money laundering, protection scams, and pretty much any other illicit way to make money. He amassed power and wealth, and to this day, nobody had taken it from him.

But that didn't stop the nightmares. Nothing could stop the nightmares. Not booze, not sex, not drugs. Sammy had tried them all. Hell, he'd tried them all at the same time. But nothing worked. At night, the demons crawled out of their graves, and he woke up with a scream banging against clenched teeth.

He flipped back the covers and slid out of bed. He wore silk boxers and nothing more. Sweat dappled the thick tangle of gray hair on his chest as he padded across the floor on bare feet and pushed back the curtain enough to see the beach outside. The moonlit dunes beckoned to him, and he debated taking a long-past-midnight stroll. Perhaps the feel of sand between his toes and the susurration of the ocean would calm his frazzled nerves. Sometimes nature worked better than any narcotic.

His phone buzzed over on the nightstand, interrupting his thoughts of getting outside and letting the breeze chase away his nighttime demons. Just a single vibration, so he knew it was a text coming through. He thought about ignoring it and taking the walk on the beach instead, but decided he should probably at least check it. Plenty of people had his cell phone number, but not many would dare to disturb him this late at night. It could be important.

The notification let him know that the text was from Taide. He tapped the screen to open the message.

A photo of Taide's severed head filled the screen.

A weaker man might have dropped to his knees with a strangled, anguished cry. But Saigon Sammy was not given to displays of weakness, not even when staring at his firstborn son's dead, blood-drenched face and rolled-back eyes. His jaw clenched, and his fist tightened around the phone, but those were the only outward expressions of emotion. Everything else stayed tucked inside.

Except for the rage. If anyone had been watching him at that moment, they would have seen the undisguised rage burning in his eyes. Grief, he could control. Rage, not so much.

His son was dead. Yes, he felt grief, and he would weep later. But the grief was unequivocally eclipsed by the fury he felt within.

The phone vibrated in his hand as a call came through. The screen notification said the call was from Taide. But of course, that could not be true. Would never be true again.

He tapped the screen to accept the call and raised the phone to his ear as he answered with a tight, terse, "Yes."

"Quattro?"

Sammy didn't recognize the voice on the other end of the line. "Who is this?" he demanded. "Aside from a dead man, that is."

"Seems to me," the voice said, "that the only dead man you need to be worried about right now is your son."

Sammy clenched the phone so hard it threatened to break apart in his fist. "I still didn't get your name, motherfucker."

"Not really that important," the voice said. "But if you feel the need to call me something other than 'motherfucker,' you can call me Rabid."

Sammy didn't waste time with any more threats. He just got right down to business. "Okay, Rabid. I figure you killed my boy to send me a message. Let's hear it."

"The message is simple, really. You're in bed with the Crimson Cross."

"Not sure how that's any of your damn business."

"It's not," Rabid replied. "You want to work with those Soviet dogs, knock your socks off. But Uday Tunicov has his pack of mongrels snatching up girls on Rene Perelli's turf, and that cannot stand."

"Perelli could have reached out to me," Sammy said. "I would have looked into it."

"She doesn't want it looked into. She wants it stopped."

"So, to stop the trafficking, she started a gang war. Always thought she was smarter than that." Sammy grunted disdainfully into the phone. "Guess I was wrong."

"It's only a war if you retaliate," Rabid said.

"She killed my son and cut off his head. Of course I'm going to retaliate."

"Actually, *I* killed your son and cut off his head."

"She gave the order."

"And you have two more sons," Rabid rasped. "Keep your commie cocksuckers off our turf or bury all your kids. Consider yourself warned."

The line went dead.

Sammy snarled a curse and hurled his phone against the wall above the headboard. The shattered pieces rained down on the beach bunny, startling her awake with a shocked cry. The thin covers fell away as she propped herself up on all fours, looking around bewilderedly. For a brief moment, he considered taking her that way, hard and rough, venting his rage and grief on her soft, supple body. But the temptation passed as quickly as it came.

"Get out," he hissed at her through clenched teeth. "Get out *now*."

She didn't argue. Just gathered up her clothes and fled. Sammy had no doubt she would occupy another rich man's bed by tomorrow night. Not that he cared. Bump-and-dump bitches like her were a dime a dozen. She could be replaced with a snap of his fingers.

He wished he could replace his son that easily.

But while he might not be able to replace him, he *would* avenge him. Saigon Sammy was not a man who forgave sins committed against him. He would have his reckoning.

There would be a reckoning with the man called Rabid for pulling the trigger.

There would be a reckoning with Rene Perelli for ordering Taide's execution.

And there would be a reckoning with Uday

Tunicov for his reckless, unleashed stupidity that had cost Taide his life.

Sammy silently cursed himself for getting into bed with the Crimson Cross. Clearly, that had been a mistake and one that had now cost him dearly. Very loosely associated with the regular Russian mafia—more of a splinter group, really—the Crimson Cross was notorious for their savagery and willingness to do whatever it took to make money, but they utterly lacked any sense of the unspoken codes and decorum that governed the more established criminal organizations.

If the regular Russian mafia was a purebred, pedigreed, showstopper of a canine, then the Crimson Cross was a drooling, snaggle-jawed, junkyard mutt with more muscles than brains.

Sammy rarely made mistakes. That's how he had survived so long in this dirty business. But he had made the mistake of believing he could control Uday Tunicov and his motley crew of marauders, a ragtag assortment of losers and gutter thugs mixed with a handful of ex-Spetsnaz soldiers.

Sammy had been warned by his Canadian counterparts that the Crimson Cross had made a mess of Montreal and basically been kicked out by the Grekov Gang, who severed their association with them. Tunicov and his boys had migrated south, crossing the border into New York to set up shop in Albany. Sammy had ignored the warnings from his Montreal compatriots and formed an alliance, letting Tunicov operate on his turf in exchange for a sizable chunk of the profits.

There'd been two simple rules.

Number one: stay on Quattro turf.

Number two: no human trafficking.

Now, if Rabid was telling the truth, Tunicov had violated both rules by straying onto Perelli turf and snatching up girls.

And Taide had paid the price.

Which meant Rene Perelli and Uday Tunicov had to die.

CHAPTER 1

GABRIEL ASHER LET his fingers brush against his holstered Heckler & Koch HK45 Tactical pistol. The gun felt comfortably familiar, almost like an extension of his hand. It also felt cold, deadly, and ready to kill. The same could be said for the man who wielded it. Asher had long ago made peace with who he was, but that didn't mean he always liked it. He had tried to walk away from it all before, but found himself dragged back into the killing game. Sometimes he yearned for something more.

Something beyond all the blood and bullets.

Sitting next to him in the shotgun seat of the SUV, his best friend and fellow warrior, Malakai, asked, "You ready for this rodeo?"

Asher used night-vision binoculars to survey the large farmhouse in the distance, only partially visible through the trees they had used to conceal their approach. The house was huge and retrofitted with luxury rather than utility in mind. Intel from the two analysts back at the Church—the new headquarters of the resurrected and redesigned Black Talon unit—indicated that Uday Tunicov, leader of the Crimson Cross, was holed up here, away from the city, for a few days. It provided Asher and Malakai a prime opportunity to strike, and Senator Olander had sanctioned the mission. She was the head of the Senate Intelligence Committee and the overseer of the Black Talon program. In other words, the one who called the shots.

Uday Tunicov was involved in a wide range of offenses, including but not limited to narcotics, black market weapons, and human trafficking. The drugs and the guns might have been enough to put him on Black Talon's radar, but the human slavery had sealed the deal and put him in the crosshairs. It was the reason he was about to die. Something about using people as cattle and currency provoked a deep anger in Asher and sparked an intense hatred for the Crimson Cross leader.

Asher lowered the binoculars. "Ready as I'm gonna be."

"You not feeling it?"

"I'm fine."

"I can handle this one alone if you want to sit it out," Malakai offered. "Been a while since I activated my one-man army mode."

"Yeah, that's not gonna happen," Asher replied. "I'm not going to sit on my ass while you have all the fun."

"Fine with me," said Malakai. "But it doesn't seem like this is fun for you anymore."

"Was it ever?"

"Depends on your definition of fun."

They double-checked their equipment, making sure rounds were chambered in both their rifles and sidearms. Their tactical vests bristled with spare magazines and grenades.

They didn't have an exact count of how many guards roamed the grounds of the farmhouse, so they were prepared to engage with a small army of Crimson Cross shooters, if that's what it took to reach Tunicov. They were headhunting the big dog and would rain hell down on any of the cannon fodder mongrels that got in their way.

"Let's rock 'n' roll." Malakai opened the door and vacated the vehicle, stepping out into the night air, trading the warmth of the cab for the cold of winter. His breath plumed like dragon smoke as he snapped his Heckler & Koch UMP45 submachine gun to his shoulder and moved through the woods, silent as a ghost.

Asher followed. He usually favored a Franchi SPAS-12 combat shotgun, but this strike would presumably require a larger ammo capacity, so he'd opted for a suppressed M4 Carbine sporting a red-dot scope. The thirty-round magazine was packed with brass, ready to crank rounds into enemy targets. Which he would do without hesitation. He might be getting sick and tired of all the killing, but that wouldn't stop him from dropping scumbags face down in the dirt.

There was no security fencing around the farmhouse, just the usual wooden post-and-rail fencing found on all farms, this one completely encircling the fifteen acres that made up the rural estate. Tunicov relied on roving patrols for his defensive security when he was out here in the country.

That was a mistake, and they intended to make him pay for it with his life.

Asher and Malakai took out the perimeter patrols without incident, their weapons chugging out hushed shots that sent bullets tearing into temples and foreheads. The Crimson Cross sentries were cooking in hell before they knew what hit them.

They cut across a professionally landscaped cobblestone path that snaked through shoveled snowbanks, the salt used to melt the ice crunching softly under their boots. They slid up the concrete steps to the wide porch that extended, southern-style, across the entire front of the house, and took up positions on either side of the front door. Intel from the Church indicated Tunicov did not employ cameras out here at the farmhouse, but you could never be sure. Asher and Malakai had decided to breach immediately before any unknown cameras spotted them.

They moved with the smooth precision of men who had worked the kill-zones together for a long time. Malakai's UMP45 chewed apart the lock, and Asher kicked open the door, going in low and fast. He sensed rather than saw Malakai tight on his six.

Two men, casually dressed, guarding the foyer, got caught off guard. They reached for pistols holstered on their hips as soon as they realized they were under attack.

Asher and Malakai announced their arrival with lead and flame. Asher smoked the guy on the left with a double tap to the head while Malakai ventilated the other one with a pair of bullets in the chest. Both bodies tumbled to the marble floor. In the assassination game, that was known as a good start.

A target appeared in the hallway to their left. Asher pivoted and drilled him through the sternum. Beside him, he heard Malakai hitting the trigger, putting bursts into bad guys. He didn't need to turn and check on the results. If Malakai was shooting, the targets were as good as dead.

More guards swarmed toward them. Both warriors dropped to their knees as incoming rounds whistled overhead. They took out the trash with sustained, sweeping salvos that carved into abdomens and tracked upward across chests and throats before exploding foreheads.

Another wave of Crimson Cross soldiers boiled into the foyer, which was quickly becoming an abattoir. Asher and Malakai had come prepared to face a small army, and that's exactly what they were doing. Uday Tunicov might be a subhuman piece of garbage, but he was definitely well protected.

The fight devolved into a close-quarters scenario. Asher emptied the M4's magazine and then transitioned to his HK45 pistol. In his peripheral, he saw Malakai do the same and glimpsed his partner zapping one of the Russians right in the chest with his FNX-45 sidearm. Neat little hole going in, big messy hole coming out.

Asher's next shot split open a target's chin like a hatchet and drilled deep into the skull.

No mercy, no hesitation. Just kill or be killed.

Swift, brutal, unflinching action was required to survive against these Russians, many of whom happened to be ex-military. Spetsnaz, to be exact. The Church's intel had been crystal clear on that particular nugget of information.

This wasn't the first time Asher had clashed with ex-Spetsnaz killers. They were tough as nails, bred for war, not civility. It often seemed like they felt no pain, as if they had endured such grueling conditioning that they had become numb. Still, Asher had found their reputation to be somewhat exaggerated. Damn straight, they were good, but they weren't *that* good.

Which he proved by shooting another one in the face.

"Watch your six!"

He heard Malakai's warning and spun to find a hulking specter closing in from behind. The goliath had to be at least six feet eight, with linebacker shoulders and close to three hundred pounds of solid muscle that seemed carved from granite. Oddly enough, he wielded no weapon. But then, his giant fists looked like oversized sledgehammers capable of splattering the average person to pulp with a single blow.

But Asher wasn't your average victim. He had tangled with plenty of muscle-monsters like this before and knew they all went down when you put a bullet in them.

He swung the .45 into play.

The hulking Russian moved swifter than seemed humanly possible for someone his size, surging forward and slapping aside the barrel so that Asher's shot missed by inches, sizzling past the ribcage. The blow sent the weapon flying from his hand. It sailed through the air, landed on the marble floor, and skidded up against the wall.

"Son of a bitch!"

A quick glance at Malakai revealed his partner was tied up with his own henchmen. No help there. He reached for the rifle sling to bring the M4 back into play, but before he could complete the action, a hard palm-strike hammered his chest. It felt like he'd been rammed by a rhino, and he went down hard, landing flat on his back. The air exploded from his lungs. He thought about scrambling for his fallen .45 but knew the Russian would be all over him before he got there. He could reach for his knife, but there just wasn't enough time.

The giant reached down for him, and Asher opted for the weaponless approach.

His foot shot out and slammed the bulky guy in the gut. He gave it everything he had and felt the son of a bitch's intestines collapsing around his buried boot heel. Maybe he'd get lucky and rupture something.

The Russian coughed out a painful gasp and staggered backward two steps, clutching at his punished abdomen.

It was all the room Asher needed. He powered to his feet and went to work with his fists. His strikes landed with tactical precision, but the big bastard might as well have been wearing body armor. An irritated grunt was the only indication he had even felt the blows.

The Russian hit back with a cinderblock-sized fist that caught Asher in the side of the head, hard knuckles cracking against his left temple with stunning impact. Before he could shake it off, the goliath grabbed him by the scruff of the neck with his left hand while he cocked the right fist back to deliver a facial pounding. Asher knew if that blow landed, it was going to break bone and take him out of the fight. Malakai would be left to fend for himself.

No fucking way.

Asher moved with a speed that belied the starbursts

pin-wheeling through his skull. He reached over his shoulder, snagged the fingers clutching the back of his neck, and pulled them apart like he was tearing open a bag of potato chips. They snapped and broke at the knuckles, ripping an agonized bellow from the giant's lips.

Asher brought his knee up fast and hard into the guy's gonads. Then he did it again for good measure, pulverizing all the tender stuff in the groin region. The bellow turned into a straight scream, high and shrill, like a little girl.

Malakai had stopped shooting. Asher knew time was ticking against them. Uday Tunicov would be fleeing out the back door if they didn't corner him soon.

Asher heaved a knee into the Russian's balls one more time, a crushing blow that made things crackle and crunch. As the behemoth staggered backward, clutching his punished privates, Asher scooped his HK45 off the floor and shot him through the neck. Blood spurted from blown carotids.

"You done screwing around over there?" Malakai called out as the giant toppled to the floor with a heavy crash.

Asher shook his head like a wet dog to clear away the remaining cobwebs that still clung to the inside of his skull from the son of a bitch's punch. "Don't you have more people to shoot?" he asked.

"Guess I'll have to do the shooting since you can't hang onto your gun."

Asher ignored the good-natured jab and swept his gaze over the blood-drenched foyer, littered with twitching, bullet-mutilated corpses. Testimony to their lethal skills and marksmanship.

He looked at Malakai. "Let's go find the head honcho."

"Thought you'd never ask."

To their right was a set of double doors. They knew from the pre-mission briefing that the doors opened into a large study. It was where they expected to find Uday Tunicov holed up with his most trusted guards, exact total unknown.

Just like before, Malakai's UMP45 chewed apart the lock. He kicked open the door just enough to toss in a flash-bang and then rolled to the side. Panicked shouts from inside the study were drowned out a few seconds later by the grenade's detonation. The double doors rattled in their frame so hard that the hinges nearly shook loose.

The two assassins entered the room side by side, gunning down targets incapacitated by the ear-rupturing bang and the blinding, seven-million-candela blast of magnesium-powered light.

Asher could hear someone—Tunicov, presumably—hiding behind the mammoth desk, screaming orders at the guards. The words were in Russian, but Asher could make out things like "shoot," "kill," and "stop," sprinkled with some colorful foreign obscenities.

The bodyguards tried to comply, tried to recover their bearings after the flash-bang fucked them all up, tried to get their weapons back on track—but it was useless. Asher and Malakai mowed them down.

Back-to-back, they picked off targets like they were at a carnival shooting range. Their bullets hammered through bodies and ripped through heads, sending blood spraying into the air like a crimson mist. Asher felt the .45 grow lighter with every round expended.

After the slaughter came the silence.

Asher slammed a fresh magazine into the HK45 as Uday Tunicov slowly rose to his feet from behind the desk, trembling with a mix of fear and rage. There was undoubtedly a weapon secured under the desk, but Tunicov seemed uninterested in reaching for it.

Still, no point in taking unnecessary risks.

Asher shot him in the right shoulder.

Then the left shoulder.

He damn sure wouldn't be reaching for any weapon now.

Tunicov fell backward into his chair, teeth clenched in pain as blood poured from the bullet holes.

"Gotta tell you," Malakai said, walking forward after completing his own magazine exchange. "Given the numbers at your disposal, I expected this to be a little harder."

The Russian gang leader glowered at them, his angry eyes flicking back and forth between the two assassins. "What are you doing here?"

"What do you think?" Asher replied.

"Maybe he thinks we're just some really determined Jehovah's Witnesses," Malakai said.

Tunicov didn't respond. Just sat and stared and bled.

Asher gripped his pistol tighter as he studied the commie bastard and thought about all the innocent women who had been traded at his command. As far as he was concerned, white slavers were worthless, heartless, subhuman pieces of crap. He had plenty of regrets about his killing ways over the years. But he had never once regretted putting a bullet in a sex trafficker.

He wouldn't regret putting one in Tunicov, either.

"Is this about revenge?" the Russian asked. "Did I take someone you care about?"

Asher nailed him with a steely, unrelenting gaze. "It's about justice."

Tunicov straightened up, trying to muster as much dignity as he could with bullet holes in both shoulders and facing down two executioners. "I will not beg," he said stiffly. "If you are going to kill me, then get on with it."

"Don't tempt me," said Asher.

"You've got no idea how tempting it is," Malakai added. "I'd really like to pull the trigger and be done with this."

"But you have information we want even more," Asher continued. "That's your stay-out-of-a-casket ticket. Tell us about the latest shipment, tell us where we can find the girls, and you get to keep wasting God's good air."

Tunicov sulked and sighed and then said, "Those stupid whores? Really? That's what this is all about?"

"Yeah," Asher replied. "That's what it's about. And if you keep calling them whores, it could be detrimental to your life expectancy."

"Start talking," Malakai growled at the Crimson Cross flesh trader. His FNX-45 pistol hung low at his side, but it could be brought into play in less than a heartbeat. He would happily blow Tunicov's balls off one at a time if that's what it took to rescue the lost girls before they were sold off to the highest bidder.

The Russian gangster was savvy enough to know that his death was a done deal if he kept his mouth shut. Nothing about Asher and Malakai's demeanors gave the impression they were bluffing. Tunicov had chosen to play this cutthroat game, and he knew the cold, hard, unforgiving rules. No point in bucking them now, especially with a pair of guns aimed at him.

"My downtown club on the southside." Tunicov spat the words, clearly angry that he was being forced to say them. "They should be there by dawn."

"How many?" Malakai asked.

"How many what? Girls or guards?"

"Both."

Tunicov started to shrug, then stopped and winced as the movement caused fresh pain in his shoulders. "I do not know all the details. I have underlings who handle that. But if I had to guess, probably five or six girls, three or four guards."

Malakai nodded. "Thanks." He raised his pistol, finger touching the trigger.

"Now wait a minute!" Tunicov's eyes widened. "You said you would let me live."

Asher brought his own .45 to bear, aligning it with Malakai's weapon, and aimed at the Russian's forehead. "Yeah, we lied."

They didn't waste any more time. They had what they needed. Quick kill, two to the chest, two to the head. Heart blown apart, brains scrambled like hash, and just like that, Uday Tunicov, leader of the Crimson Cross, was scrubbed off the board.

Mission accomplished, damn straight.

The room reeked with the coppery scent of spilled blood and the acrid burn of gunpowder. Smells they were all too familiar with.

Asher glanced over and saw Malakai giving him a crooked grin. "What the hell are you smirking about?"

"Just wondering if you brought a rose with you."

Back in his freelance days, Asher had marked his kills with a white rose, his personal calling card. He would drop it in a pool of blood, a symbol of innocence lost, or some poetic shit like that. In hindsight, he honestly wasn't sure why he did it.

Asher shook his head. "Haven't done that since I killed Peter Perelli."

"Still regret that one?"

"I turned his wife into a widow and took away a child's father. I'd be a heartless monster if I didn't feel some kind of regret."

"He deserved it," Malakai replied. "Peter Perelli was not a good man."

"I know he deserved it," Asher said. "But that little girl didn't. If I could take it all back, I would."

Malakai holstered his gun. Around them, dead men twitched from muscle spasms as their bodies slowly accepted the lethal trauma inflicted upon them. "Your truce with Rene Perelli still holding?"

Rene Perelli had ascended to the criminal throne left vacant when Asher assassinated her husband, proving herself to be a ruthless ice queen that was in sharp contrast to the demure, subservient vibe she had projected when Peter had been alive. With the power of the Perelli crime organization behind her, she had come gunning for vengeance. Asher managed to turn the tables and could have—maybe *should* have—killed her, but allowed her to live with the understanding that he would not be merciful again.

"If she comes at me again, she knows what will happen," he replied, holstering his own gun. "She stays away from me. I stay away from her. It's working so far."

"Let's hope it stays that way," Malakai said. "I'd hate to see you make that kid of hers an orphan."

Yeah, Asher thought. *That would suck.* But he knew that sometimes in war, the children suffered and paid the price for their parents' sins. He said, "I don't think she'll go back on her word."

"Hate to break it to you, pal," Malakai replied. "But all truces break, eventually."

Asher didn't reply. He didn't want to think about a coming day when he might have to put a bullet in Rene Perelli.

Instead, he looked around at the gunned-down gangsters strewn across the floor. He'd never been one to relish killing, but the sight left him feeling colder than usual. He and Malakai destroyed vermin, the marauders, the predators of society. There was a dark honor, a hard code, in what they did, but all that slaughter still took its toll. At least, it did for him.

They had ridden with the Reaper tonight but once again managed to dodge the Grim One's scythe. But he knew that unless they found a way to leave the killing grounds, that life-snuffing blade would reap their souls, eventually. Asher felt a weariness seep into his bones. All he wanted to do was close his eyes, drift off to sleep, and for just a few hours forget who—and what—he was.

But that would have to wait. They still needed to rescue the girls.

At dawn, death would come riding once again.

Because in the end, death always wins.

CHAPTER 2

SHORTLY AFTER DAWN, they hit the club.

The four Russian gangsters inside got gunned down before they even realized they were under attack. It was a short-lived massacre, Asher and Malakai delivering controlled bursts of auto-fire that riddled the men with bullets. The commie goons never got off a single return shot.

The quartet of corpses was christened with a dark-red barbed wire cross tattoo on the side of their necks, the symbol of the Crimson Cross gang. Maybe some people found it intimidating, but Asher and Malakai were not those people. As far as Asher was concerned, the tattoo looked more like a target than anything. Shoot the cross, kill the man.

There were five girls locked in a storage room in the back of the club, all bearing signs of abuse and all drugged up, arms pierced and punctured with needle marks. They were too strung out on forcibly injected narcotics to even know they were being rescued.

"Call Olander," Asher said, looking at the young

victims with sympathetic eyes. "We need a cleaning crew for this mess and medical attention for these girls."

"Got it," Malakai replied.

Asher sleeved sweat off his face as his friend made the call. Senator Paula Olander was not only the head of the Senate Intelligence Committee, she was the person directly responsible for resurrecting the Black Talon program and transforming it from a ruthless, conscienceless black ops kill-squad that hunted down assassins who walked away from the Company—like Asher had once—into something with a more noble purpose. With Malakai and Asher as the tip of the spear, Black Talon was still very much an assassination unit, but without the unleashed, out-of-control, mad-dog quality of its previous incarnation under the leadership of Colonel Macklin.

Macklin had murdered Asher's wife and framed it to look like a suicide. Asher had paid him back by snapping his spine and cutting his throat in a grisly back-woods showdown. There were days Asher wished he could dig the bastard up and kill him all over again.

Senator Olander personally oversaw nearly all of Black Talon's operations, and between that and her political duties, how she found time to sleep was anyone's guess. She had exerted her powerful influence to suspend the Company-issued kill orders against Asher and Malakai in exchange for their returning to the fold. So that they would not be looking over their shoulders for the rest of their lives and to protect the women they loved, they had agreed to work for her.

Generally speaking, Asher respected the senator, but respect and trust were not the same thing. He had learned long ago that in this kill-or-be-killed game, trust came at a premium. He trusted Malakai, Larissa, and Shiomi. Everyone else he kept at arm's length.

Malakai made the call, speaking cool and calm, keeping things vague despite the phone's military-grade encryption. "The job's done. Place needs a good cleaning, and someone should check on the packages in the back." A pause. "Copy. ETA thirty minutes for the cleaners." Another pause. "Copy. We'll catch our ride once the cleaners arrive and meet you at the Church at 0900."

Malakai ended the call, dropped the phone back in his pocket, and went to check on the girls, who still looked zombified and traumatized. God only knew if they would ever recover from their hellish ordeal, and even if they did, the therapy bills would be huge.

Asher went outside and stowed his carbine in the SUV, enjoying the fresh winter air, ready to head upstate into the Adirondack Mountains, to the Keene Valley log cabin he now called home. Above, dawn continued to creep across the sky in tendrils of pink and purple. Police sirens wailed in another part of the city, the good guys waging the everlasting war against the bad guys.

Asher leaned a hip against the SUV and thought about Larissa. In the world of blood and darkness in which he lived, she was his salvation, a shining light, the anchor that kept him from tumbling too far into the abyss. Ultimately, she was the reason he killed, because he killed to keep her safe. And when the killing was done, and the bodies were stacked, she was the one he went running home to.

He wanted to run home now, not go to the Church for a debriefing. That had been one of the best parts about being a freelancer—no paperwork. Now, after every hit, there were reports and meetings and analyses to suffer through. But if he didn't play the game, the kill order against him could be dropped back in place like a guillotine coming down, and that would put Larissa in harm's way, which was completely unacceptable. He might be willing to gamble with his own life, but not hers.

Malakai came out and put his Heckler & Koch UMP45 in the back of the SUV next to Asher's M4. They waited in silence, the morning sky brightening with every passing minute, until the cleaners and medics arrived. Then it was time to go. They were no longer needed here. Their job was to kill. Other people handled the aftermath of the killing. They were all just cogs in a machine.

A machine oiled with blood.

Asher inhaled deeply, drawing the cold air into his sinuses. It made him yearn for the icy mists of the mountain valley he called home and the woman who waited for him there. Then he exhaled, long and slow, trying to release his tension and moodiness.

"Let's get the hell out of here," he said.

"You don't have to tell me twice," Malakai replied and climbed into the SUV. They left the death-strewn club behind them and headed for their rendezvous with the chopper that would fly them back to the Church.

The ninety-minute flight from the hustle and bustle of New York City to rural Maryland gave Asher plenty of time to be alone with his thoughts.

That wasn't always a good thing.

The Church was a place where saints and sinners once mingled, but now only killers crossed its once-sacred threshold. The only angels that gathered here now were the angels of death.

The Church had started its existence as an actual church, a Gothic stone structure built in Garrett County, Maryland, in the early 1900s. It had been abandoned in the woods outside the small town of Friendsville, forsaken by the Methodists who owned it, and they had been only too happy to sell it to the federal government. Senator Olander had the place renovated and retrofitted to serve as a secluded operational base for the Black Talon program. From the outside, it just looked like a regular church, albeit one not open for *business*. Inside, however, while it still retained some of the vestiges from its former purpose, it provided space for Black Talon's small support team to work. Instead of candles and crucifixes, there was a command center.

Asher stood outside and stared up at the cathedral. It was tall, steepled, the stone tower stabbing up into the sky like it was reaching for heaven. The stained-glass windows displayed angels and demons locked in mortal combat, which was Olander's idea of a joke. Asher wondered if there were any other churches in the country that had bulletproofed their stained-glass windows. Seemed sacrilegious, somehow.

Between the two of them, Malakai possessed more faith than Asher did, because he had been raised by a Bible-thumping—albeit abusive—father. Asher believed in God in some vague, undefined way, but it was not necessarily a religious faith, and certainly not one that required a sanctuary and sacred rituals. Mostly, he just hoped that the next life would be a hell of a lot better than this one.

"Every time we come here," Malakai quipped, "you act like a vampire afraid to cross the threshold."

"Just ready to get this debriefing over with so we can go home."

"I hear that, but we really should take showers first."

"Are you hitting on me?"

Malakai grinned. "Not what I meant when I said I had your back."

The two assassins headed down to the Church's basement, which was equipped with a small living space, including a pair of bunks, showers, and a kitchenette. They stripped off their gear and washed up before heading upstairs to the main sanctuary where the support personnel worked.

Asher's eyes shifted to one computer analyst in particular. Vesper was his favorite, and if he were being honest, he knew that if it wasn't for Larissa, there would probably be something between him and the pretty, young, spunky analyst with the permanently bemused and charming smile.

"Well, well," Vesper greeted. "Look what the cat dragged in." The pair of black, rectangular glasses she wore would have looked geeky on anyone else, but on her they somehow enhanced her simplistic beauty, showing off her dark eyes that were framed by silky black hair that stopped just above her shoulders. She wore a light blue blouse that was tight enough to accentuate her ample chest.

Yeah, she was a looker, all right. But he loved Larissa, and nothing would change that.

"*Look What the Cat Dragged In* was the name of a

Poison album," Malakai said. "It's old, it's cliché, and if that's the best you've got, I'm very disappointed in you, Vesper."

"Hate to break it to you, but you're not the first man I've disappointed, Malakai."

"Touché."

Asher gave her a friendly smile. "Hey, Vesper."

"Hey, yourself, Gabriel. Mission complete, I take it?" Her eyes scanned him up and down, and she clearly liked what she saw. Unlike him, she didn't bother hiding her attraction, even though she was well aware nothing would come of it. He'd made his love for Larissa very clear.

"Tunicov terminated."

"That's good news," said Vesper. "One less Russian mobster to deal with."

"There'll be more," Malakai said. "There's always more. Bad guys are like cockroaches. You can never kill them all."

"Any trouble?" Vesper asked.

"Nothing unusual," Malakai replied. "Just shot a lot of people in the face and called it a day."

"Somebody's gotta do it, right?" Vesper smiled. "Might as well be you two."

Somebody else chose that moment to join the conversation. Somebody Asher really could have done without. Easily his least favorite person in the Black Talon program.

"Gentlemen." Wyatt Paltrow was a sharp-dressed man who looked more like a politician than an analyst. His impressive head of wavy brown hair had that perfectly messy look that only a high-priced salon could provide. By contrast, the stupid bowtie he insisted on wearing was always crooked. "A pleasure to see you again."

Can't say the feeling is mutual, Asher thought, but kept it to himself. Instead, he just gave a curt nod of acknowledgment. "Wyatt."

"How are you cowboys doing today? Stacking up the bodies, increasing your kill count, adding notches to your guns?"

"Sure," Malakai replied. "And I've got room for one more, so don't piss me off today."

"Wouldn't dream of it." Wyatt let out an obnoxious, squeaky chuckle and dropped into his chair. He spun around and faced his computer terminal, giving them his back. Asher resisted the urge to walk over and snap his neck. Not only would it enrage Senator Olander, but it violated his own code to not kill innocents. Wyatt was a pretentious prick, but that didn't mean he deserved to die.

"We're just here for a debriefing," Asher said. "Then we'll head for home."

"Sure, okay, whatever." Wyatt shifted in his chair, which produced an irritating screech. "Thanks so much for letting me know."

Asher reconsidered his decision not to kill the guy. It wasn't just his annoying nature, either. There was just something off about Wyatt. The way he spoke, the way he acted, his overall vibe...It was all just a little weird for Asher's taste. He generally tried not to judge a book by its cover, but when it came to Wyatt, he had a gut feeling, and he had learned long ago to trust his instincts. They sometimes steered him wrong, but most of the time they were dead on the money.

Then again, what were his instincts when stacked

against the Black Talon screening process? This was a black ops program, with hits being conducted on American soil. Everyone who joined the support team was intensely questioned and subjected to a battery of tests and intrusive background checks that made a visit to the proctologist seem like the epitome of privacy. You didn't just stroll up to the Church, knock on the door, submit a résumé, and say, "Please hire me."

In theory, there should be no way for somebody shady to slip through the cracks and infiltrate the operation. But then, Asher knew there was *always* a way. Clandestine government programs throughout history had been littered with moles.

It didn't help that Wyatt was constantly giving Vesper lustful looks, stripping her with his eyes every chance he got. Maybe she didn't notice, but Asher certainly did. He was experienced at reconnaissance, accustomed to watching people, and knew how to evaluate their facial expressions, nonverbal cues, and subtle hints of intention. So it was clear to him that Wyatt had designs on Vesper. He talked to her more than anyone else. Made excuses to visit her workstation, where he always managed to "accidentally" touch her, usually on the arm or shoulder, but sometimes managing to brush her leg. A man clearly interested in mixing business with pleasure.

Asher knew it couldn't be jealousy on his part—he loved Larissa, not Vesper—but he also knew that he *liked* Vesper and didn't appreciate seeing her harassed by a toad like Wyatt. But he kept his feelings to himself. He had not even told Malakai about them. His emotions on the matter were too easy to misinterpret, and he didn't need his best friend questioning his devotion to Larissa.

"You're awfully quiet over there, cowboy," Wyatt said. "Busy thinking about all the blood you've got on your hands?"

"We can't all just sit on our asses, all safe and comfy behind a keyboard," Asher replied. "Somebody has to do the dirty work."

"Somebody has to sit behind a keyboard too," Wyatt retorted. "You trigger-pullers can't do your job without us computer geeks. We go together like hands and gloves, socks and feet."

Asher didn't even try to hide his disdain. "I was doing just fine killing bad guys before you came along."

"Come on, don't even try to put rose petals on a turd, Gabe. You were nothing more than a rogue freelancer doing hits for the mob. Not exactly something to brag about." Wyatt swiveled around in his chair and smirked at Asher, twirling a pen between his fingers like a kid playing with a fidget toy. "But hey, what do I know? I'm just a safe and comfy analyst."

"What you are is an asshole." Asher was tired after a long night on the killing grounds and didn't feel like holding his tongue or mincing his words. "And ridding the world of assholes is kind of what I do. You might want to remember that while you're busy pissing me off."

"Holy shit." Wyatt looked genuinely stunned. "Did you...did you just *threaten* me? You can't do that."

"I just did."

"Olander will hear about this."

"Ask me if I give a shit."

Asher wasn't worried about what Wyatt might say

to the boss. The little cry-ass could go whine all he wanted. This was a black ops unit, not a kindergarten class with *Be Kind* banners written in crayon on the wall. There was no human resources department to complain to if your feelings got hurt, no safe spaces or trigger warnings or political correctness. That kind of bullshit had no place here, because it interfered with Black Talon's singular goal.

Exterminating bad guys.

Wyatt could bitch and moan all he wanted, but at the end of the day, Senator Olander—if she even bothered to listen—would tell him to shut up, suck it up, and get back to work. Hotshot computer analysts could be easily replaced. They were a dime a dozen at any respectable university. But assassins with the top-tier skills of Asher and Malakai were not. All the data sifting and intel interpretation in the world was worthless without gunslingers to take care of business once the analyzing was over and the targets identified.

Still, Wyatt could be a thorn in his side if he really put his mind to it. Despite their simmering hostility toward each other, the guy was still a part of the Black Talon team, someone handpicked by Senator Olander herself. And credit where it was due, Asher couldn't deny Wyatt was good at his job, maybe even better than Vesper. Too bad he was such a tool about it.

But this was a killer's game, and Wyatt wasn't a killer, not by any stretch of the imagination. Hell, Asher wasn't sure the guy possessed enough gumption to swat a mosquito. Of course, that didn't mean he wasn't a snake in the grass, and Asher fully intended to keep a close eye on him. There was just something off about the guy.

I don't trust him, Asher thought. *Then again, I don't trust most people.*

Larissa. Malakai. Shiomi. These were the people he trusted, the ones who had earned his loyalty, those he would lay down his life for. Everyone else he considered capable of compromise. A jaded, cynical outlook for sure, but it had kept him alive so far. Better to be a living, breathing cynic than an optimist with a nice coffin.

Asher would keep Wyatt in the crosshairs, watching, waiting. If he turned out to be harmless, then no harm, no foul. But if he proved to be some kind of devil-serpent in the Black Talon garden, he would take him out quicker than you put down a rabid dog.

Then he would reload and do the same to anyone who threatened him or the people he cared for.

CHAPTER 3

THE DEBRIEFING at the Church lasted until just shortly after noon. Asher and Malakai then said goodbye to Vesper, pointedly ignored Wyatt, and headed out to find a bar for a post-mission drink before heading home for some well-earned R&R. They had dodged death, taken out the trash, and lived to talk about it. That deserved a couple of beers.

They found an out-of-the-way western-themed roadhouse and took a table by a railing that overlooked the dance floor, a few people bopping to some southern-fried rock from the jukebox even at this early hour. A buxom waitress in tight jeans and a flannel shirt, with honey-brown hair tied back in a ponytail that reached down to the middle of her back, came over to take their order. The heels of her cowboy boots clicked on the wooden floor.

"You guys have Red Dog?" Malakai asked.

"That beer from the nineties?"

"That's the one, yeah."

"Uh, no. Why would we have a beer that hasn't been popular in thirty years?"

"Because it's damn good, that's why."

She smiled, showing perfectly white teeth. "Guess I'll just have to take your word for it."

"How about a couple of Buds then?"

"Now that I can do."

The waitress sauntered off to fetch their beers, hips swaying in a manner that could have been natural or could have been exaggerated to catch their attention. Not that it mattered, because they were both going home to something even better. Asher missed Larissa something fierce, and he had no doubt Malakai was feeling the same about Shiomi.

The Budweisers were delivered a few minutes later, the brown bottles refreshingly cold. Malakai took a long pull and sighed contentedly. "Man, that hits the spot." Then he looked at Asher. "So...you want to talk about the burr under your saddle?"

"What do you mean?"

"Don't play dumb with me." Malakai took another swig and then swiped the back of his hand across his lips. "I'm not just your partner. I'm your fucking friend, and I know when something's eating at you. Please tell me you're not fretting about those Russian dirtbags we waxed last night."

"Not exactly."

"Because those assholes deserved every bullet we gave them."

"Sometimes I think we all deserve a bullet." Asher raised the bottle to his lips. The beer was cold but tasted flat, like wet ashes in his mouth. Or maybe that was just his mood making it seem that way.

Malakai shook his head. "God, you're a gloomy bastard sometimes."

He's not wrong, Asher thought. He was self-honest enough to admit that he sometimes spiraled down into a dark, depressing place. In the past, that spiral had been fueled by Jack Daniels, but that wasn't an issue anymore. He had gotten better since Larissa came back into his life, but the fact that he was forced to continue to kill in order to keep her safe often weighed on him like a heavy cross.

"You know how it is," he finally said.

"Sick of the life?"

Asher nodded. "I went freelance for a reason. I didn't want the Company's chains around my neck anymore. Then I wanted to just put away my guns and live a normal life with Larissa. But now here I am, right back where I started, wearing those damn chains again."

"And it's making you ornery."

Asher arched an eyebrow. "Ornery?"

"I'm not just another pretty face with a pistol," Malakai replied. "I know big words too."

"Not sure ornery counts as a big word."

"See, there you go, being ornery again."

"Maybe I just need to go home. Haven't seen Larissa since Olander tugged on our leashes to take out Tunicov."

"Home will do us both some good, no doubt. God knows I'm looking forward to seeing Shiomi."

Asher took a drink, then used his thumb to wipe away some droplets of condensation on the bottle, almost like a believer rubbing rosary beads. "I'm just getting tired of doing what we do."

"I hear you," Malakai said. "But you have to remember the reason why you do it."

"I do it to keep her safe."

"Right," Malakai replied. "You do it for love. You do it for Larissa. I do it for Shiomi. It was the right decision when we made the call back then, and it's still the right decision today. Without this deal with Olander, we'd still have kill orders hanging over our heads, and Shiomi and Larissa would both be in the crosshairs right along with us."

"You ever think that maybe they would have been better off if they never met us?"

Malakai shook his head emphatically. "No, hell no, and fuck no. They were already in danger when they met us. Larissa would have been raped and killed by Giadello's goon, and Shiomi would still be hooking for the Syndicate. We made their lives better, not worse. Stop being such a morose motherfucker."

Asher knew his friend was right, but it felt good to hear somebody else say it. He also knew he was just making misery-talk over a couple of beers. Ultimately, no matter how he felt, he would stay where he was and keep doing the job to protect the ones he loved. Walking away just wasn't an option right now.

But he also knew he couldn't pull the trigger forever. Eventually, he would need to figure out an exit strategy. Staying in the killing game chipped away at his humanity, eroding it like slow-eating acid. Someday, assassinations would be carried out by robots, androids, or cyborgs, but until then, humans needed to do it, and humans paid an emotional cost. Asher knew this fact all too well. It was why he tried to walk away once before. He had lost his soul back then, and only through Larissa had he found it again. Truth was, she had saved him every bit as much as he had saved her.

"I hear you," he said. "Loud and clear. I'm bitching about something I don't really have a choice in."

"Exactly," Malakai agreed.

"Because I know what happens if I walk away from it all."

"What happens if you walk away from Talon is completely unacceptable," Malakai replied. "For us, and for Shiomi and Larissa. I'd rather kill assholes for the rest of my life than see them get hurt or dead."

They both fell quiet, and Asher knew his friend was thinking about Shiomi. Malakai loved her every bit as much as Asher loved Larissa. She'd suffered a horrible, shitty life before Malakai crossed her path, having been forced into prostitution by her father so that he could ingratiate himself with the Syndicate, a Japanese criminal organization with tentacles all across the globe that made the Yakuza look like choirboys. Malakai had gone on the warpath to rescue her from a life of slavery, killing her father in the process.

"She wants to start a family," Malakai announced.

"Damn," said Asher. "Dropping a bombshell like that is one way to get me to stop crying in my beer."

"Marriage, kids, the white picket fence, backyard barbecues...She wants it all."

"The whole shebang."

"Exactly."

Asher tried to picture Malakai playing suburban husband, attending pool parties and PTA meetings, flipping burgers, having beers with the neighbors. Truth be told, he couldn't really see it. No doubt Malakai would do whatever it took to make Shiomi happy, but the domesticated lifestyle didn't really suit him. Or at least, it hadn't up to this point.

"That appeal to you at all?" he asked. "Trading your gun for a spatula? Your sports car for a minivan?"

Malakai shrugged. "I don't know. I mean, not really, not right now anyway. But as you like to point out, we can't do this crap forever, right? All the guns and guts, it's got an expiration date. Or at least, I hope it does, for both our sakes. But right now, this gunslinger life isn't exactly conducive to raising a family."

"I hear you."

"Besides," Malakai continued, "when enemies find out you have something to lose, they start targeting your weakness. A wife, kids—hell, even a dog—can be used as leverage against you."

"That's true."

"Of course it's true. That's why I said it."

"You said it to me. What about Shiomi? You say all that to her?"

"More times than I can count," Malakai replied with a little shake of his head. "She understands where I'm coming from, understands the game we have to play. But she still gets frustrated, even angry sometimes."

"Part of being in a relationship," Asher said. "It's not always sunshine and roses."

"Yeah, well, I'm running out of rosy ways to tell her I'm not ready for all that."

"Think you ever will be?"

"Don't know. Still trying to figure that part out." Malakai drained the last of his beer and set down the empty bottle. "How about Larissa? How's she feel about this run-and-gun lifestyle?"

"It's complicated," Asher said. "More than anything, she feels guilty."

"About what?"

"About the fact that I have to kill people to keep her safe. She feels like she's trading someone else's head for hers."

"Her head is innocent. The scumbags we kill aren't."

"She knows that."

"Not enough justification for her?"

"Not enough to take away her guilt, apparently," Asher said. "The price for her safety is still paid in blood, and she doesn't like it. Just like me, she wishes we could just get out of the killing game and live a normal life."

"That day will come," Malakai said.

Good words, reassuring words, but Asher could tell his friend wasn't as confident as he tried to sound. They both knew that achieving a life of peace and solitude was most likely not in the cards for either one of them. And frankly, neither of them was sure they deserved it after the things they had done. God might forgive, sure, but sometimes karma steps in and makes sure you get the punishment you've got coming. They both lived with the raw, stark knowledge that they would most likely eat a bullet rather than die of old age. Wasting away their twilight years in a rocking chair on the front porch just wasn't the destiny men like them deserved.

Then again, sometimes *deserved* had nothing to do with the outcome.

"Maybe you're right," Asher said. "Maybe that day will come. But I don't think it's going to be anytime soon."

Malakai sighed. "Yeah, I think you're right about that." He raised his empty bottle. "To someday."

Asher clinked the necks of their bottles together. "To someday." Then he slid off his stool, grabbed Malakai's empty, and asked, "One more round before we hit the road?"

"You buying?"

"Sure."

"Can't say no to that."

Asher wandered over to the bar. The bartender was pretty in a girl-next-door kind of way, blonde hair pulled back in a ponytail, white T-shirt at least a size too small to amplify her assets and garner more tips. Oldest trick in the book.

As he set the empties down, he heard a loud commotion from the pool table located near the bathrooms. He turned his head and saw five guys gathered over there, grunting, hollering, dropping expletives, and just generally acting like your typical drunken, boorish morons. All five of them wore blue jeans and flannel shirts with ripped sleeves, like some kind of unofficial uniform. Asher could practically smell the booze from here.

"What can I get for you?" the bartender asked, flipping a towel over her shoulder.

Asher didn't answer, his attention focused on the group of buffoons. They horsed around like stupid teenagers who didn't know how to hold their liquor, swinging the pool cues as if they were the weaponized staffs used in martial arts. It was about as graceful as watching an elephant do ballet.

"Hey, yo!" one of them shouted, hair buzzed into a short Mohawk and a heavy chain necklace dangling.

"Check this out. I'm a goddamned ninja! *Hi-YA!*" He snapped his leg forward in an exaggerated kick, nearly lost his balance, and completed the mimic with a racial slur for Asians.

Asher glanced over at Malakai to see if his friend had heard. With Shiomi being full-blooded Japanese, Malakai did not generally take well to those kinds of slurs, caricatures, and mockery. Asher saw the scowl on his partner's face and knew the rudeness had not gone unnoticed.

"Hello?" The bartender waved a hand in front of his face to get his attention. "I said, what can I get for you? Want some popcorn while you watch the idiot show over there?"

Before Asher could reply, one of the men whipped a cue stick backward and smashed it into the mirror on the wall. With a *crack-crackle-crunch*, glass shards rained down in a messy heap. All five men laughed like howler monkeys, as if the vandalism was the funniest fucking thing they'd ever seen.

"Damn it," the bartender snapped. She whipped the towel off her shoulder and slapped it down on the bar, clearly irritated. "I'll be right back," she said. She spun on her heel and marched over to the cackling cretins while Asher kept watch.

"Will you guys cut your crap and stop acting like a bunch of juvenile delinquents? C'mon, Brian. How many times do we have to tell you that you and your boys are no longer welcome here?"

"Aw, relax, Nikki. Ain't no one getting hurt." Brian had red hair peeking out from beneath a backward trucker's hat and a neatly trimmed red beard to match. He wore a Hooters T-shirt under his open flannel.

"Yeah? Tell that to the mirror." She pointed at the broken glass on the floor. "Clean this mess up, finish your drinks, and get the hell out."

Nikki the bartender was small but feisty, angry fire flashing in her eyes as she stomped back to the bar. Clearly, she'd had encounters with Brian and his band of inebriated jackasses before. Asher glanced around, looking for the bouncer who should be backing her up and throwing these clowns out. He didn't see one.

"Sorry 'bout that." Nikki handed him two fresh bottles of Bud and popped the caps with the practiced ease of someone who had done it a thousand times. "There you go."

Asher dipped his head toward the pool table. "Friends of yours?"

"Just a bunch of regular dumbasses causing trouble and busting up the place. Every time they come in here, Brian and his idiot entourage get drunk and play rough. They've been banned but keep coming back." She shrugged. "Not a whole lot I can do about it."

"Where's the bouncer?"

"Called in sick."

"You want them gone?"

Nikki gave him an appraising stare. "You just gonna take on five guys all by yourself?"

Asher jerked a thumb over his shoulder at Malakai. "No, I've got help."

"That's still two against five."

"Yeah." Asher smiled tightly. "They should have brought more men." He headed for the pool table. Malakai slid off his stool and joined him.

Brian and his four sidekicks were bouncing around like chimpanzees jacked up on speedballs, swinging their cue sticks with reckless abandon, chugging beer like it was the last day before Prohibition, and just generally being obnoxious as hell. Not a single one of them seemed capable of talking in a normal tone of voice. They screamed their words, half of which were expletives.

So much for just having a nice, quiet drink, Asher thought.

Still, he wouldn't escalate this confrontation to violence unless it became absolutely necessary. He had no particular wish to hurt these drunk assholes. He just wanted them gone. They were bullies, and they didn't belong here.

Brian twirled the cue stick like a baton while two guys threw pool balls at each other and the other two faked a sword duel with their sticks. They all shuffled drunkenly, nearly tripping over their own feet. If this went to fisticuffs, Asher figured it wouldn't be much of a fight.

As he and Malakai made their way in, Asher felt composed and tried to project a non-threatening demeanor. Not really his strong suit, but he did his best.

"Excuse me, fellas."

When Asher spoke, the gang all stopped and gawked at him. They looked like they could not believe that he had the audacity to bother them. There were some grunted curse words and coarse chuckles.

Brian stepped closer. "Whoa, hold up, guys. We've got ourselves a visitor. Maybe they want to join our little party." He strutted up to Asher and gave him a stare that was supposed to be threatening. Hell, maybe it was to most people.

But Asher was not most people. He just stared back

with a cold, level gaze. "Sorry, not really in a party mood right now. Just came over to ask you to keep it down."

"Keep it down?" Brian echoed.

"That's what I said."

"What's that supposed to mean?"

Malakai answered, "We can hear you all the way from the other side of the bar. Makes it hard to enjoy our drinks and relax. Plus, you're breaking things that don't belong to you. I think everyone would appreciate it if you just dialed it back a bit."

The barely bridled fury on Brian's ghoulish face made it clear the request was asking too much. At that moment, Asher had little doubt that this confrontation was about to escalate. He sighed inwardly, but also knew he wouldn't back down from a fight. Wasn't really his style, and besides, he wasn't in the mood.

"You work for the bar or something?" Brian asked. He glanced over his shoulder to make sure his friends were still backing him up. Seeing that they were, he fixed his gaze on Asher again. "Don't believe I've ever seen you two losers around here before. You just show up and volunteer?"

"Maybe he fancies himself a cooler like in that *Road House* movie," one of the goons said with a tobacco-stained grin. "Thinks he can just roll into town and start kicking ass."

"Is that it?" Brian asked. "You think you're some kind of roadhouse-taming cowboy?"

"No," Asher replied, keeping his voice calm but firm. "I just came here for a quiet drink, and I'd like to make sure things stay quiet."

"Oh, are we ruining your good time?" Brian feigned shock. "Making too much noise for your sensitive ears?"

Asher didn't indulge him with a reply. Wasn't worth wasting his breath.

"I swear that's not our intention at all," Brian continued. "Is it fellas?" He received supportive chuckles from his pack of clowns. "That's not why we're here, not at all, so I guess we'll turn down the volume until this place is a fucking library. My apologies, stranger."

Asher felt his muscles tighten, his nerves go taut, his knuckles clench. But it was just drunken, bullying sarcasm, nothing that merited takedowns and broken bones.

Not yet, anyway.

"Thanks," Asher said.

"Just one little thing, though." Brian held up his index finger in a *wait-a-minute* gesture. "Before you tuck tail and scuttle away, would you mind buying us another round to make up for interrupting our game? You know, a small token to compensate for your rudeness."

Asher gritted his teeth. He was losing patience with these dipshits.

The mohawked guy stepped up and stood by Brian's shoulder, a half-full mug of beer in his hand. "Yeah," he said. "I'm empty." His arm shot forward, the beer flying out of the glass to splash across Asher's chest.

The assassin didn't move for a moment. Just stood there, soaked with the malty beverage. Some of the droplets had splashed up to pepper his stubbled jawline, and after several long heartbeats, he slowly reached up and wiped them away. Then he took a deep breath and looked at Malakai, whose face bore a very unimpressed expression. His friend gave him a slight nod, letting him know that it was time to take out the trash and teach these fools a lesson.

Brian's gorilla gang all laughed while Brian himself settled for a smug smile. "Yeah," he said. "I reckon that round's on you."

Asher's plan was simple.

Give 'em hell, and make it fast.

He speared Brian in the throat with rigid fingers, pulling the strike so it wouldn't crush his windpipe and kill him. Brian took the blow just below the Adam's apple and immediately vomited a splurge of bubbly booze. As Brian gasped for air, Asher drove a knee into his gut, and when he doubled over, dropped an elbow onto the back of his neck to finish him off. He went down hard, his face bouncing off the barroom floor with a meaty smack.

The rest of the pack rushed forward to defend their leader.

It was like lambs attacking lions.

Asher kicked the first one in the ribs and then spun out of the way of the second. As the guy slipped past, Asher grabbed a pool ball off the table and rocked him in the back of the skull. Not hard enough to break bone, but hard enough to put the guy on the floor with his lights out. He was going to have one whopper of a concussion when he woke up.

Asher whipped back around and returned his attention to the first guy, busy clutching his bruised ribs. A hard chopping blow to the temple sent him reeling to the floor beside the others.

Three down, two left.

Feral and pissed, they barreled forward like angry bulls.

"Let me know if you need help," Malakai quipped.

"I've got it," Asher said.

"I can see that."

The fourth guy took Asher's boot to his knee. As he crumpled, a snapping hook to the face dislocated his jaw and finished him off. He went down, banging his head off the corner of the pool table, and flopped on the floor like a rag doll.

The fifth guy looked like he considered backing out of the fight, but then changed his mind and came in swinging. Asher rewarded him with a kick to the stomach that stopped him in his tracks, and a sweeping roundhouse finished the job.

Over on the floor, Brian started to stir, shaking his head to clear the cobwebs as he climbed to his feet.

Damn, Asher thought. *Guess I should have hit him harder*.

He spotted a cue stick lying on the floor. He nudged it up onto his boot and flicked it up into his hand. He saw Malakai leaning against a post, clearly amused. Been a long time since they'd enjoyed a good, old-fashioned bar brawl.

Asher spun the cue stick like a staff as Brian approached, then lashed out, striking the man in the mouth. A tooth popped out, tumbled down his beard, and clattered to the floor. A follow-up blow hammered him in the chest like a horse kick. Brian stumbled backward several steps.

When he regained his balance, he glared at Asher

with blood dripping from his battered mouth. "You cocksucker. You're gonna pay for that."

"Somehow, I very much doubt it," Asher replied. He kept his voice taunting. He wanted Brian angry. The angrier an opponent got, the more careless they became.

"You're dead, fucker!"

As the last angry syllable left Brian's mouth, Malakai came off the post and launched a devastating roundhouse kick that smoked him in the face and pulped his nose like a splattered strawberry. He toppled like a chainsawed tree.

"You were saying?" Malakai rasped at the fallen bully.

"I had it under control," Asher said, tossing the cue stick onto the pool table.

"Guess I got tired of standing around watching you have all the fun."

"Well, thanks for having my back."

"Always."

Brian and his gang were sprawled on the floor, some splayed out, others curled up in the fetal position. None of them would be getting up anytime soon. The fight was over. Asher felt the aggression drain out of him. He'd spent last night gunning down Russian mobsters and today roughing up rude, rowdy drunks. Time to go home.

Asher and Malakai looked at the people clustered around them, the patrons who had edged closer to watch the show. They looked in awe of what they had seen, and several tossed slightly fearful glances at the two assassins, as if just now sensing the dangerous aura that neither of them could escape. They were stained by the relentless violence of their lives, and when people got close enough, they picked up on it, and it often made them afraid.

"Let's get out of here," Asher said.

"Yeah, that's probably a good idea," Malakai replied.

They stopped by the bar to pay their tab, along with some extra cash to cover the damages, but Nikki waved it away. "On the house, guys. You earned it." She gave them a warm smile and a friendly wave goodbye.

As they headed outside, Malakai said, "Well, this has been one hell of a day."

"You can say that again," Asher agreed.

"We're just magnets for trouble."

"Those assholes deserved it."

"Maybe they learned their lesson."

"What lesson would that be?"

"Never start a fight with someone you don't know."

Asher looked up at the sky. Thick white clouds filled most of it, but patches of blue showed through here and there. He felt fatigue taking hold, a combination of lack of sleep, adrenaline dump, and alcohol. He didn't regret taking time for a beer with Malakai, but he was ready to be home with Larissa.

Malakai seemed to sense his thoughts and asked, "Ready to hit the road?"

Asher nodded, feeling the weariness seep even deeper into his bones. They had a whole lot of miles to go before they could fall into their own beds. He was heading north. Malakai was heading south. Being on opposite ends of the East Coast meant they rarely saw each other these days unless Black Talon summoned them for an assignment. Neither he nor Malakai were overly sentimental creatures—at least not outwardly—but sometimes saying goodbye was a little more difficult than either cared to admit. They had saved each other's lives, *continued* to save each other's lives, and it gave them a bond of friendship, a bond of blood, a bond of brotherhood. It remained unspoken between them, but their mutual loyalty was beyond question.

There was no one else Asher would rather kill with.

Malakai was standing there with his door open, ready to slide behind the wheel. "You coming?"

"Yeah."

They climbed in, Malakai fired up the engine, and they headed for the airport with no further words between them.

None were needed.

CHAPTER 4

XIANG FUKUDA RELISHED THE SILENCE.

The world was bloated with far too many hollow, meaningless words. It showed a lack of respect that he found intolerable. Communications, actions, gestures... all should have meaning, and there should be consequences for the ones that merely prattled and preened with emptiness.

In Fukuda's world, *consequences* could usually be translated as *death*. Sometimes swift, sometimes slow and painful, but it was always there. A constant companion, an eternal presence.

Fukuda was the leader, the *kumicho*, of the Japanese criminal conglomerate known as the Syndicate. He was the head of the hydra, the manipulating force behind a thousand tentacles that called Japan home but reached across the globe.

He emerged naked from the sunken, heated whirlpool within the bathhouse of his ornate mansion, unashamed of his lack of clothes or the toll the advancement of years had taken upon his body. Misty condensation from the hot water filled the room, wreathing his body like the ghosts of his dead ancestors.

There were ten guards ringed around him. One stepped forward to drape a silk robe upon his moist body, and all acknowledged their master by easing their heads forward. Their bows were subtle, stoic, much like Fukuda himself. He knew every guard by name and trusted them as much as he trusted anybody. They had been personally selected from the hundreds of warriors he had at his beck and call, and each and every one of them would gladly lay down their lives for him.

He cinched the robe around his waist with a tight knot. He was tall, still trim, and deceptively strong for a man of his advanced years. He had refused to allow his life of luxury to make him soft. He moved lightly on the balls of his bare feet as he stepped toward the guards arrayed by the door. He fixed his eyes on one of them.

The guard immediately bowed again. "Master."

"Has he arrived?" Fukuda inquired.

"*Hai.*"

"Bring him to me."

———

Tucked away in a back corner of the Syndicate lair, the man being summoned—Yemon Nakano—rested in a meditation room, eyelids closed, his breathing calm and rhythmic. He was alone, in silence, and much like his master, he preferred it that way. He sat on the tatami floor with his legs bent in the traditional Japanese manner—*seiza*—and remained calm and resolute as he waited to be escorted before the *kumicho*.

He sensed, rather than saw, someone's approach.

Knew, if he cared to look, that he would see the person's shadow printed on the rice paper of the shoji door. A moment later, the door slid open, and a man's voice disturbed the calm.

"The *kumicho* demands your presence."

Nakano slowly opened his eyes. Or rather, *eye*, because only the right one remained. It moved in its socket, falling on the guard, who was wearing what appeared to be a very expensive suit. The empty left socket remained hidden behind a black eyepatch. Very softly, his voice like silk on razored steel, Nakano acknowledged the man's announcement with a simple, "*Hai.*"

His eye had not been taken by force or by accident. It had been surrendered, a gift freely given. For all who wished to join the Syndicate, a sacrifice was required. Some gave wealth, some gave family...Nakano had given his flesh, the pain of loss, the agony of severance. He had done it in front of Xiang Fukuda many, many years ago, earning the man's respect, and with the respect came the prestige and power that only someone like Fukuda could bestow.

He had done the deed with the same blade he now carried. His fingers lightly grazed the handle as he rose from the floor. He remembered Fukuda watching impassively when he made the incision, slicing the cutting edge across the ocular orb until it burst, spilling milky fluid down his face. Without flinching, Nakano had reached into the bloody cavity, plucked out the deflated eyeball, and presented it as a raw, twitching offering.

"Good," Fukuda had said. "Very good. You are now *ishinokanbase no kami.*"

The stone-faced god.

"Nakano-san?"

The guard's voice drew Nakano back to the present. And in that present, he found the additional layer of demand and insistence in the man's tone offensive. He reacted by whipping his arm forward, the blade sailing across the room in a silver blur, light reflecting off the honed steel. It pegged the wall next to the guard's head. A deliberate miss. The assassin meant to shock and warn, not to kill.

Startled, the guard turned to look at the blade quivering in the wall beside his ear. It had missed by less than half an inch. The guard slowly stepped away from the door, the look on his face making it clear that he would not dare to disrupt the stone-faced god again.

The usually stoic Nakano allowed himself the indulgence of a thin smile. Some lessons were easy to teach.

He tugged on the sleeves of his suit, ensuring the fit was snug, proper, and precise. He respected scant few people in this world, but Fukuda-san was one of them. He would not stand before his master looking slovenly. Satisfied, he exited the meditation room and followed the now nervous guard to the center of the mansion, where Fukuda's private lair nestled.

It was a cavernous room, complete with a waterfall, exotic plants, and landscaped lighting. Traditional Japanese music played softly from hidden speakers, merging with the burbling of the water tumbling over the rocks to create a sonic palette that fostered relaxation and peace.

But Nakano knew that peace and relaxation were

not the reasons he had been brought here. Those were not his specialties.

He bowed to his master. "I apologize for my tardiness," he said. "I was preparing for whatever task you have for me."

Fukuda sat poised behind a long, ancient-looking desk fashioned from cherrywood, braced by a quartet of guards on each side. There was a single chair positioned in front of it.

"No apology necessary," Fukuda replied. His deep, raspy voice sounded like there was a fire burning in the pit of his throat. "Men of your particular talents require time to prepare."

"I would be of no use to you if I did not."

Fukuda motioned for Nakano to come and sit across from him. "Make no mistake, *ishinokanbase no kami,* you are extremely useful to me."

As he came forward, Nakano considered the reason he had been summoned. Primarily, his duties and expectations revolved around the central tenets of *kill and destroy*. He was the instrument. Fukuda-san would provide the target.

"I am in need of your services," Fukuda said once Nakano had taken a seat. "The kind of task that can only be trusted to someone like you."

"Tell me the name, and it will be done."

"Shiomi."

Nakano nodded. It was the name he had expected to hear. "I know her. Or rather, I know *of* her. Her name is often whispered among our ranks."

Fukuda leaned back, hands clasped together in front of his chest. "She betrayed us. She has turned her back on the Syndicate."

"I have heard."

"Are you also aware that she killed one of our leaders, her own father?"

"Tanaka-san."

Fukuda nodded. "Yes."

Actually, Nakano had heard that an assassin named Malakai had killed Tanaka, not Shiomi. But correcting Fukuda would result in his tongue being ripped from his mouth with a pair of hot tongs. Besides, Malakai had killed Tanaka *because* of Shiomi, so she might as well have pulled the trigger—or rather, thrown him to the sharks and tossed him a grenade—herself. Either way, she had sealed her fate. Nakano now knew what his next assignment would be.

"Killing one of our own is an act that cannot go unpunished," Fukuda said. "We have already ignored Shiomi's transgression for too long. I am asking you to do what is necessary."

"It shall be done." Nakano's razored whisper of a voice was cold, dispassionate. "You have my word."

"Go to America," Fukuda commanded. "Hunt down Shiomi and those associated with her and finish them. I want a message sent that defiance of the Syndicate results in death."

"I understand."

"Just be aware that her associates might be more capable than you are accustomed to."

Nakano expressed his surprise with an arched eyebrow.

"You heard me." Fukuda leaned forward, hands now clasped on the desk in front of him. "Shiomi is protected by assassins, two of the best, I am told, who now work for a covert organization."

"Black Talon?"

The shadow of a smile appeared on Fukuda's face. "Your knowledge of our enemies is impressive."

Nakano bowed slightly to acknowledge the compliment. Truth be told, there had been ripples in the underground when Black Talon had been resurrected and repurposed, and he had paid close attention. The previous version of Black Talon had been a pack of ruthless mad dogs solely focused on tracking down and exterminating Company agents who went rogue. This new incarnation, however, allegedly featured two elite assassins who hunted the criminals of the world.

People like Fukuda.

People like Nakano.

People like the Syndicate.

"We have been struck a blow," Fukuda said. "We must strike back. Shiomi's continued existence is a blight on our reputation, one that makes us look weak. And as you are well aware, weakness is unacceptable. You will go to the United States and meet with a contact who will assist you in locating the ones responsible for Tanaka-san's death. When you find them, you will make them pay for their transgressions."

"The assassins," Nakano said. "Do we know their names? Who they are?"

"Asher and Malakai."

Nakano nodded. He knew of them. They had a reputation as being very good, maybe even the best. "And our contact?" he asked.

"Samuele Quattro," Fukuda replied. "The one they call Saigon Sammy."

"The mobster from New York." Nakano was not surprised to hear that the Syndicate and the mob were allied. He knew the Japanese crime lords often subcontracted work to other criminal organizations. It was simply the nature of the game, another strategy in expanding the Syndicate's global stranglehold.

Fukuda nodded. "Quattro will provide you with what you need to hunt down your targets. Weapons, transportation, intel...everything you require to accomplish your objective will be provided once you reach the US."

Nakano filed the information away and gave it no more thought. If Fukuda said the necessary intelligence and equipment would be there, then they would be there. The assurance might as well have come from the lips of God, as far as Nakano was concerned.

"Do you have any questions?" Fukuda asked.

Nakano shook his head.

"Very well." Fukuda made a dismissive motion with his hand, signaling that the meeting had come to an end. The time for talking was over. Now it was time to commence the mission and focus on exterminating his targets. Nakano rose, bowed, and headed for the door.

Face stoic, Nakano had almost reached the exit when Fukuda addressed him again.

"Ishinokanbase no kami."

The sharpness in his master's tone gave Nakano pause. He stopped in his tracks and peered over his shoulder, acknowledging Fukuda's call.

"Do not underestimate these men," the leader of the Syndicate warned. "That would be a grave mistake on your part."

Nakano nodded slightly. *"Hai."*

He resisted the urge to defend himself. He had not acquired his legendary status as an elite killer by underestimating opponents. Especially two Black Talon assassins with the reputations of Gabriel Asher and Malakai. They had both survived against overwhelming odds, even when outgunned.

No, they were not like the others he had hunted. They were far better. Maybe even better than him. Time would soon tell.

Nakano relished the coming confrontation. Easy kills brought their own pleasure, but they paled in comparison to the challenge of hunting prey that was also a predator. He, Malakai, and Asher shared many similarities, but they were different in one very crucial way.

They killed because it was their job.

Nakano also killed because it was his job.

Difference was, he enjoyed it.

Time to enter the shadows and dance with death once again.

CHAPTER 5

WASHINGTON, DC, was a city teeming with American history, featuring iconic sights such as the White House, the Washington Monument, the Tomb of the Unknown Soldier, and the US Capitol building, to name just a few. Even the most disconnected and jaded individuals sometimes found themselves awestruck in the presence of the symbolic stone and steel architecture, the sacrificial heritage infused into every corner and crevice.

Without a doubt, this was a city where decisions were made that could reshape not just the country, but the very world itself. Senator Paula Olander, chair of the Senate Intelligence Committee and overseer of the ultra-covert Black Talon program, was very much aware of this fact because she frequently made such decisions herself.

Since Talon's resurrection under her command, the focus had been on native threats, the targets limited to American soil. But she had plans to broaden the war zone in the future and take out targets on foreign shores when necessary. Those kinds of decisions could change the geopolitical landscape in the blink of an eye.

She strolled toward the Oval Office in her dark-blue business suit and sensible shoes—leave the posh dresses and high heels for the young upstarts more interested in social media clicks than actual politicking—and with a no-nonsense look etched on her face. Her eyes weren't ice-queen cold, but they were definitely on the frosty side when she glanced at the people she passed. She knew she had few friends in these hallowed halls, but she had something even better—respect. Behind her often brusque demeanor was a woman who got things done.

The Syndicate had tried to blackmail her with salacious photos from her youth, but she was still standing. Her husband had betrayed her and been assassinated for it—by the very assassin who now worked for her, no less—but she was still standing. The dirty, gutter-wallowing politics of the Senate chamber had tried to ruin her, but she was still standing.

Hell, put that on my goddamned gravestone, she thought. *Still standing*.

She stopped at the desk in the outer Oval Office and informed the secretary that she was here to see the president. She did not tell her why, because it was none of her damn business, and the secretary knew better than to ask. You didn't last long as the president's secretary by being nosy.

"Yes, the president is expecting you," the portly woman said. "Should be just a moment. Please have a seat."

"I'll stand, thanks."

The secretary gave her a sour expression. Clearly,

she felt standing up while waiting to be seen by the president was an unsatisfactory breach of White House protocol, but she didn't press the issue. She might not know that Olander commanded a black ops wet work program with lethal gunslingers at her disposal, but she clearly sensed that the senator was not someone to be trifled with. Olander resisted the urge to pat her on the head and say, "Smart girl."

It didn't take long before the secretary announced, "The president will see you now."

Olander nodded and entered the Oval Office. She did it casually, as if walking into her own living room. The famous office had impressed her at one time, long ago, but now it was just a place to rattle off updates to the most powerful man in the world. In the end, it was just a room with some nice furniture in it, symbolism be damned.

"Good evening, Paula."

The president was a stern-looking man in his late sixties. Despite his age, he had looked somewhat youthful when he won the election. Or at least, the wear and tear had not been so evident. Now, two years into his second tenure, his hair was more gray than black, and the smooth skin of his face had given way to the deep, craggy fissures of constant worry. He handled the pressure well—nobody could deny the man was cool in a crisis—but it had definitely taken a physical toll.

He wore a black suit that made him look like he was on his way to a funeral, but a red and blue striped tie added some color. His stern face softened as he shook Olander's hand. "Thanks for coming."

"Of course, Mr. President."

He had told her repeatedly that she could call him

by his first name when they were in private, but she never did. To her, being friendly and being friends were not the same thing.

The president gestured toward the sofa. "Have a seat."

They were not alone, and Olander settled her eyes on the other person in the room.

The young man in a dark-blue suit rested cross-legged on the couch. He was well-tanned, his hair slick with carefully applied gel, his teeth the kind of dazzling white that only comes from dental cosmetics, and there was an American flag pin fastened to his lapel. Olander supposed some easily impressed folks would find him dashing, but she wasn't one of them. Took more than nice clothes and a fake smile to move her needle. In her considerable experience, that kind of perfect, pristine exterior often hid a dirty, blackened heart. She took an immediate disliking to whomever this person was.

The president introduced him. "This is Brody Anderson, a new congressman from Vermont." His tone was flat and matter-of-fact. Olander easily picked up on the cold inflection. The president clearly wasn't smitten by Anderson's suit-and-smile façade either.

For his part, Anderson seemed unperturbed by the fact that the president didn't seem to want him here. Olander wondered why the rookie congressman was allowed to stay. This meeting was way above his pay grade.

This was a highly classified sit-down to discuss the latest mission of a black ops program that only a few people were aware existed. Black Talon—and the people who operated it—were one of the country's best-kept secrets. There was no way Brody Anderson had achieved need-to-know status in his short time in the political arena.

Anderson gave her an ingratiating smile. "Pleased to meet you, Senator."

Olander nodded curtly, took a seat, and looked pointedly at the president. "I take it you and the congressman were just finishing your conversation so he can leave?"

Anderson chuckled. "Not exactly."

Why is this annoying little fool here? He belongs at a school board meeting, not a classified briefing.

"Not exactly...*what?*" Olander said, eyes narrowed to show her growing disapproval with his presence. It had been a while since she took such an instant dislike to somebody. The look she gave him could have peeled flesh from bone.

"Not exactly leaving," Anderson replied smugly.

"Care to explain why not?"

The president answered, "Congressman Anderson will be joining our inner circle." He said it the same way he might have said he was having a root canal with a power drill.

"The hell he will," said Olander. "Absolutely not."

"I'm not asking, Paula," the president replied. "I'm telling you."

"I have complete oversight of the program."

"You have *operational* oversight," the president corrected. "And that has not changed, I assure you. But *I* decide who needs to know about Black Talon and who does not."

"More people sitting at the table means more risk for my people."

"People?" Anderson scoffed. "They're assassins. Subhuman at best."

"Shut up, Brody." The president's voice was firm, commanding. It gentled when he said to Olander, "I'm aware of that, Paula. But it doesn't change anything. Despite your objections, which are duly noted, Mr. Anderson will be joining us."

"I think I'm at least owed an explanation."

The president stared at her but didn't say anything. She returned his gaze without blinking, waiting him out.

But it was Anderson who finally spoke. "If it makes you feel better, Senator, it really wasn't up to him."

Olander glanced at the congressman. "You want to run that by me again?"

"You heard me. The president didn't have much of a choice."

Olander made eye contact with the president again, then shifted her focus back to Anderson. "Care to explain?"

"Sure," Anderson replied, reaching up to adjust his tie. "I'll keep it short and simple. The bottom line is, I happened to overhear a few things regarding your little off-the-books program and decided that I could offer some input into how things could be better handled."

Olander tried to decide whether she wanted to just punch the pretentious prick in the face a few times or wrap her fingers around his fucking throat and throttle the life out of him.

The president cut in, dropping a truth bomb. "Congressman Anderson threatened to blow the entire program by going to the press if he wasn't brought onboard."

"So...he heard something he shouldn't have and decided to compromise the safety and security of the United States by blackmailing the president and the overseer of a black ops kill team." She shot Anderson a withering look. "You're an absolute imbecile, you know that?"

The congressman gave her a mega-wattage smile. "No offense taken, Senator."

"No? That's unfortunate, because offense was definitely intended."

Anderson chuckled as if Olander had just told a joke instead of insulted him. "No, seriously, there are no hard feelings. Truth is, if Black Talon is everything it's rumored to be, then I truly believe my input will be valuable in steering the future of the program. Once you see what I have to offer, what I bring to the table, I think you'll dial back your distaste of me soon enough."

"I'd rather fuck a cobra."

His smile never wavered. "Really? Because I heard you were more into dogs and donkeys."

She gave him the same look she would give someone who had just vomited all over her favorite pair of shoes. It was steel and venom in equal measure.

Anderson leaned back in his chair, clearly unfazed. "I understand that look scares a lot of people around here," he said. "I assure you, I am not one of those people."

Olander glanced at the president. "How mad will you be if I throat-punch him? I hit him hard enough, he'll never be able to speak again. I'd be doing the world a fucking favor."

"Try to play nice," the president replied.

"Not really my forte."

"She doesn't know how to play nice," said Anderson. "Too much time spent with mad dogs. Speaking of which, I want to make it very clear to you, Senator, that I am extremely uncomfortable with unleashed aggressors killing people in the name of this country."

Olander snapped, "Who said they're *unleashed*?"

"Enough," the president said. His eyes drifted across Brody once more, clearly unimpressed, and then settled on Olander. "You didn't come here for a dick-measuring contest with a rookie who will have to learn the hard way not to mess with you. You came here to tell me about the mission. So go ahead, tell me what happened."

"We took out Tunicov at the farmhouse. No survivors."

"How many dead?"

"Cleanup crew reported thirty casualties."

"Good god." The president shook his head. "Sometimes I can't believe just how good those two guys are."

"Asher and Malakai are the best."

"Clearly."

"Wait a minute." Anderson leaned forward. "Did you say thirty casualties? As in, thirty people were killed?"

"Correct," Olander replied. "That's what I said. Try to keep up."

"Two guys killed forty people?" The congressman glanced at the president. "Good god is right. And you're okay with this?"

"I'm fine with it," the president replied. "The problem has been neutralized. Uday Tunicov was a very bad guy, and he will no longer be a problem."

"He was affiliated with the Russian mob, right?"

Anderson nodded, as if answering his own question. "Which means he was barely a drop in the bucket. Someone will replace him by tomorrow, if not sooner. If we accomplished anything by taking him out, it wasn't much."

"One assassination at a time," Olander said.

"More like thirty assassinations at a time," Anderson retorted.

"Whatever it takes."

"That's what I'm afraid of."

Their argument abruptly halted when Vice President John Steinbeck entered the Oval Office. As the VP, he commanded respect simply by the inherent authority of his position. But even if he had not been the United States' second-in-command, Steinbeck was the kind of man who dominated a room when he walked in. Tall, good-looking, with a confident air about him. The media cameras loved him, and he had been an absolute hit on the campaign trail.

"My apologies for being late," the vice president said.

The president waved it away. "No worries. Have a seat. Paula was just giving us an update."

"Right." Steinbeck stepped past Olander and Anderson and sat down near the president. It was the kind of subtle power play the man excelled at. "I heard Black Talon completed another successful mission, taking out Tunicov and those Crimson Cross bastards."

The president nodded. "You heard right."

Steinbeck looked at Olander. "Nice work, as always."

"Thanks, but Asher and Malakai did all the hard work. We'll give them some downtime, then move on to our next targets. We have several threats on our radar that we think could be removed...under the right circumstances."

"I'm sure those circumstances can be arranged."

"Glad you feel that way."

Olander was just feeding his ego. She had full operational control of Black Talon, sanctioned by the president. She didn't need Steinbeck's blessing to do a damn thing. But he liked to feel in control, even if the power was just an illusion, so she made sure to say the right words at the right time. There was nothing to gain by making the vice president of the United States feel inferior to a senator. Even though Steinbeck's position was more symbolic than anything else, better to have him as an ally than an enemy.

"What exactly do you need?" the president asked.

"Same as always," Olander replied. "Permission."

"Permission to do what?" Steinbeck asked.

"Whatever is necessary."

The vice president looked thoughtful. "You mean terminate whoever you want."

"We're an assassination unit," Olander said. "Not a charity service."

Steinbeck turned to the president. "You still find this acceptable?"

"Having second thoughts?" the president asked. "Been listening to Congressman Anderson too much lately?"

"Not at all," Steinbeck replied. "Just making sure you don't have buyer's remorse."

"Not at all," the president said. "Even if you believe that Black Talon is evil—and to be clear, I do not—it must be considered a *necessary* evil. Sometimes we must use lethal force in order to keep this country safe."

Anderson spoke up. "If we are willing to engage in assassinations to achieve our objectives, then we are no better than our enemies."

"Don't be a naïve idiot," Olander snapped. "Our enemies kill innocent people. We don't. Asher and Malakai have never put a single bullet into anyone who didn't have it coming."

"Killing is killing," Anderson said.

"If you believe that, you really *are* a naïve idiot."

"And here I thought we were a nation of laws."

"And here *I* thought that you were someone ready to be inside this particular circle," Olander said with acidic sarcasm. "Clearly, I was wrong. Maybe you should scurry on out of here and let the grownups talk."

Anderson's eyes flicked over the president and vice president, seeking some kind of support. But all he received were blank faces and stony silence.

He shook his head, grunted disapprovingly, and stood up. "I can't sit here and listen to this bloodthirsty macho bullshit masquerading as national security anymore. I'll see myself out."

He exited the Oval Office like a spoiled child who didn't get their way. Olander half expected him to slam the door on his way out.

"He has no business being involved with Black Talon," she said once he was gone. "He clearly doesn't have the stomach for what we do."

"Not everybody is cut out for this business," the president agreed. "But as I already explained to you, our hands are tied on this one. He gets a seat at the table or he runs to the press, and I don't think anyone wants that."

"He's just worried," Steinbeck said.

Olander looked at him. "Worried about what?"

"Worried about how far we're willing to go."

"We're not rogue agents," she said. "Asher and Malakai may be top-tier assassins, but they adhere to a set of principles."

"Maybe," Steinbeck conceded. "But the fact of the matter is, you pretty much blackmailed them into working for us. They're only doing our dirty work because if they don't, we'll put kill orders on them again. So let's not delude ourselves into thinking they believe in the cause."

Olander said nothing. She couldn't really dispute the point because there was a whole lot of truth to it. She honestly believed both her gunslingers *did* believe in the cause, but it was becoming clear that both of them would be happy to walk away. Asher more so than Malakai, but they both yearned to be free of their leashes.

"No country lasts forever without getting some blood on their hands," the president said. "And the US is no exception."

"If Congressman Anderson doesn't understand that sentiment," Olander said, "then it's dangerous to have him in the inner circle. He can't be trusted."

"It's too dangerous *not* to have him in the fold," the president countered. "If he went to the press with what he knows, all our careers are over."

"I'm not sure that's necessarily true," Olander replied. "But I'm not worried about my career. I'm worried about my men. I think Anderson should be removed immediately."

"Removed? As in..." The president let the unspoken question dangle.

"No, I don't mean we terminate him. Black Talon isn't in the business of targeting innocents, not even jackasses like Anderson. I just mean he should be kicked out of this need-to-know club."

Steinbeck held up his hand. "Now hold on just a minute. Anderson might not be the toughest or smartest guy in DC, but I can vouch for him. He's one of the good guys, and if you give him a chance, I think you'll find he brings something to the table."

"He's a dog begging for attention, and we're giving it to him," Olander said.

"Your voucher," the president said to Steinbeck. "What are you basing it on?"

"You have my word that he's a good guy."

"Your word? That's it?"

Steinbeck looked nonplussed. "I would think that's enough."

"Let's hope you're right," the president said. "Because, if not, we're royally screwed."

"I'll talk to Anderson, make sure he understands the lay of the land, tell him to keep his emotions under control." Steinbeck gave a little shrug. "He'll be fine, I promise. Just leave him to me."

"He's your responsibility," the president said. "Make sure he doesn't fuck us all."

Steinbeck arched his eyebrows at the uncharacteristic vulgarity, but then dropped them back in place and nodded. "I've got him." He stood up and looked at Olander. "Again, nice work dealing with Tunicov."

"Thank you."

Steinbeck nodded again, once to her, once to the president, and then headed for the door. As he exited the Oval Office, Olander wondered if he was up to the task of handling Brody Anderson. Because if not, she would handle the rookie congressman herself. Anderson might have qualms about the assassination games that played out in the shadows, but those *games* were too vital to national security to let him hijack them for political points.

Seeing her eyes follow the VP, the president said, "Don't let any of this bother you, Paula. Steinbeck will keep Anderson off your back. Black Talon is yours and yours alone. I wouldn't have given it to you if I didn't trust you with it. Run the program as you see fit."

I intend to, Olander thought. *And God help anyone who gets in my way.*

CHAPTER 6

VICE PRESIDENT STEINBECK caught up to Anderson in the hallway as the congressman headed for the exit that would take him to his car. The VP made sure there was no one within earshot as he stepped up and tapped Anderson on the shoulder.

"Brody. Hold up a minute." He said it gently enough not to offend, but firm enough to make it clear it was not a request. He felt like a teacher about to reprimand a troublesome student.

Anderson stopped and faced Steinbeck with a loud, annoyed sigh. "Whatever you've got to say, can you make it quick? My car is waiting."

Steinbeck scowled at the young congressman's borderline-blatant disrespect. *Who the hell does this little prick think he is?* He seriously considered giving Anderson a sharp tongue-lashing right here in the halls of the White House to remind the insolent son of a bitch of his place in the pecking order, but then decided to let it go. Not because he was the bigger man, but because he just didn't feel like wasting his breath.

"I need to talk to you," Steinbeck said. "Won't take long."

"It can't wait?"

Steinbeck narrowed his eyes and tightened his jaw to convey his rising irritation. "If it could wait, I wouldn't have chased you down."

"Okay, fine. What is it?"

"Do you have any idea what you did back there?"

"Back where?"

"Don't play cute with me," Steinbeck warned. "You know what I'm talking about."

Anderson had the good sense to look abashed. Maybe it was nothing more than an act designed to deflect the VP's rising anger, but the color drained from his face, and his tone lost its antagonistic edge as he replied, "I'm sorry, but I have my principles. You know that."

"You're right, I *do* know," Steinbeck said. "That's why you threatened to expose the Black Talon program."

"The American people have a right to know what their country does in the dark, under the cover of *covert operations*." Anderson injected some steel back into his voice as he added, "You think I became a politician to succumb to corruption and conspiracy?"

Steinbeck waved away the justification with a scoffing noise. "Spare me your self-righteous bullshit, Brody. If you were really sincere about your precious principles, you would have leaked Black Talon to the press instead of blackmailing us to be brought on board."

Anderson shrugged. "Maybe you're right. But at least there's somebody in the room now with a conscience, someone who wants this country to be better, do better. I want to bring change from the inside, and if that means standing up to people like Senator Olander, you, or even the president...Well, then, I guess I'll do what I have to do."

"Aren't you just an idealistic little dickhead," Steinback said. "This town is going to eat you alive. Because believe me, throwing around threats like 'I'll do what I have to do' isn't the best way to enjoy longevity in the political arena."

"Now *that* sounds like a threat to me."

"No, just some free advice."

"I didn't ask for any."

"Yeah, well, here's some more," Steinbeck said. "You need to cool your jets when you're dealing with Black Talon."

"Okay, listen, I'll grant you that I shouldn't have stormed out of the briefing," Anderson replied. "Getting verbally abused by that old bitch was really starting to piss me off, and my temper got the better of me."

"Your little walkout looked like a temper tantrum. If you think the president is impressed, you're very, very wrong. Plus, you gave Olander the win. You need to play smarter than that, Brody."

"I hear you, all right? Won't happen again."

"It damn well better not," said Steinbeck. "Trust me, you do not want to cross swords with Olander and Black Talon. Mess with Paula, and more often than not, she'll leave you shivering in your expensive shoes. That lady plays rough."

"Doesn't it bother you that there's a powerful senator out there with a ruthless kill team at her disposal?" Anderson asked.

"Asher and Malakai are not mad dogs, you know. They both follow a code. Hell, Asher even has a name for his. He calls it the Assassin's Prayer."

"Well, isn't that just goddamned poetic."

"The point is, neither of them is just going to gun down whoever Olander tells them to. Doesn't work that way. In fact, as part of their agreement to resurrect Black Talon, they reserved the right to refuse targets."

"I still don't like it."

"You don't have to like it. You just have to accept it."

"Look, I know that you're willing to sit back, not make waves, and just let the chips fall where they may, but I see things differently."

"The way you see things is irrelevant. You might have forced your way into the room with your little blackmail stunt, but let's get one thing straight—you're not running the show."

"Paula Olander has too much power," Anderson said. "Certainly too much power for a senator. And we both know that power corrupts. It's not a far stretch to imagine her using Black Talon for personal gain. You'll forgive me if I'm concerned about her unchecked authority to kill whoever she decides needs killing."

"It's not unchecked," Steinbeck countered. "Olander still runs the targets by the president."

"Has he ever told her no?"

"Not that I'm aware of."

"Exactly. Like I said—unchecked." Anderson shook his head. "Clearly, you and the president trust her and approve of what Black Talon does, but I refuse to stand by and let our country become the very thing we say we stand against."

Steinbeck let out an exhausted sigh. Anderson was trotting out a classic *I can do it better* politician speech. Full of patriotic rhetoric but laced with shovelfuls of his own particular brand of bullshit. Steinbeck found it woefully naïve, nauseating, and, quite frankly, offensive.

"Listen," he said. "You just don't understand how the game is played. You're still new. Give it some time. The game has been like this since long before me, long before you, long before anyone still left alive, and that's how it's going to be played long after we're gone."

"Maybe it's time for the game to change." As Steinbeck glared at him, Anderson added, "Maybe it's time for somebody to knock the damn pieces off the playing board so we can have a new game, a better game."

"Go home," Steinbeck said, dismissing the congressman. "And think long and hard about your next move. High and lofty ideals will only get you so far. There are some battles you just can't win."

He didn't wait for Anderson to reply. This conversation was over. He spun on his heel and walked away, irritated. He could tell that Anderson was going to be a thorn in his side, and it pissed him off. Who the hell did the greenhorn congressman from the Green Mountain state think he was? First time at a Black Talon debriefing and he acted like a gutless jackass.

Anderson wanted to talk about knocking off game pieces, but as far as Steinbeck was concerned, anyone who threatened Black Talon risked finding themselves taken off the board. Steinbeck supported the program, believed in the program, trusted the people involved in the program, and he would not allow it to be dismantled from the inside by a troublesome rookie.

Maybe Anderson was right. Maybe some pieces *did* need to be knocked off the playing board.

Starting with Anderson himself.

CHAPTER 7

ASHER AWOKE to find Larissa's hand resting on his chest, fingers lightly grazing the hard muscles there, her warm body snugged up against him. He had slept for nearly twelve hours straight, but didn't feel the urge to get up. He was comfortable in bed with the woman he loved, and that was as close to heaven as he needed.

He slid his hand down the curve of her back and pulled her close for a kiss, pressing his lips to hers. She responded with a soft smile and shifted even closer, her smooth skin moving with satin friction against his.

Asher felt his passion stir. They'd been away from each other for too long.

She smiled as his hand glided lower, following the contours of her buttocks. A moment later, the smile turned to a soft moan as she trembled under his touch. Her long blonde hair fanned out across the pillow and seemed to glow in the morning sun seeping through the window blinds. She made no protest when Asher pulled the sheets away from her, letting the light dance over her naked body. No protest, either, when his lips nuzzled her slender neck.

"Now that's a good way to wake up," she murmured.

"I can wake you up some more," Asher offered.

"Definitely." The look in her blinded eyes was sensual and sultry.

He touched her again, saying nothing, letting his hands do the talking.

She quivered, but managed to gasp out, "Sure you're not too tired?"

"For you? Never."

"Well, then..."

She let the rest go unsaid as she rolled on top of him, her lips crushing his with growing fervor, mouth flowering open so their tongues entwined. She moved against him, above him, finding his core, his need, *her* need. They made love slowly, lingering on each and every sensation, feeling no reason to rush to the end, content to be together in an intimate reminder of what they had in each other.

Lost in the moment, neither heard the bedroom door swing open. Nor did they hear the shuffle of paws on the carpet. What they could not ignore, however, was a full-size dog jumping onto the bed. Chubbs, the German shepherd that had replaced Larissa's last seeing-eye dog, let out a sharp bark and stuck his cold nose in the small of Larissa's naked back.

She yelped and rolled off Asher. He groaned in good-natured disappointment.

"Chubbs," he said with a wry grin. "You really know how to ruin a damn good morning."

Larissa smiled and patted his chest. "We can finish later. It'll be worth the wait, I promise."

"It always is." Asher kicked away the covers where they had tangled around his legs. "I'll go dump some cold water on my lap and then make us some coffee."

He donned some sweatpants and moccasin-style slippers, but no shirt, and headed out into the kitchen. The hickory cabinets and granite countertop were immaculately clean, and the appliances were organized and shiny. For a blind woman, Larissa cleaned better than most sighted people Asher knew.

Looking out the window, he saw the morning sun sparkling on the last remnants of the early-spring snow. This high in the Adirondacks, winter didn't really call it quits until late April or early May, and some of the locals claimed to have seen snowflakes on the Fourth of July once or twice. Asher figured that was a tall tale, a local legend, but he couldn't be sure.

He glanced up at the sheer rock bluff that rose a hundred feet behind his house and wrapped around the sides of his property in a horseshoe shape. It was one of the reasons he had purchased this particular place. The cliff served as a natural barrier, protecting him on three sides. In the front, the west branch of the Ausable River cut a wide swath parallel to the road, so the only access to the house was over a narrow wooden bridge.

Asher wasn't foolish enough to believe he couldn't be attacked here, but the cliff and river made it difficult. Any assault team would either need to rappel down the bluff, ford the fast-flowing water, or risk a direct frontal strike via the bridge.

That was his life. There was beauty—both the woman in his bed and the rugged nature around him—

but danger too. He doubted it would ever be any other way. For that matter, he wasn't even sure he knew *how* to live any other way.

He watched chickadees flit among the pine boughs at the base of the cliff and tried not to let his penchant for melancholy ruin a perfectly good morning. Maybe he wasn't exactly living the American dream, but things could be a whole lot worse. Hell, not all that long ago, they *had* been worse. At least now he wasn't drinking like he used to, and there was no Company kill-squad headhunting him.

By the time he had whipped up two cups of coffee, Larissa had strolled into the kitchen wearing a fluffy bathrobe loosely knotted around her waist and some of the fuzziest slippers he had ever seen, her hair tied back in a loose ponytail. She looked raggedy, but it was a sexy kind of raggedy. The robe gaping open at the top and showing a lot of cleavage helped. It made him want her even more.

Damn you, Chubbs. Can't believe I got cockblocked by a dog.

He put the cup of coffee in her hands, and she drank deeply with an exaggerated, appreciative slurping noise. "Ah, nectar of the gods," she sighed.

"That's what I say when I pour some gunpowder in my whiskey," he said.

"You pour gunpowder in your whiskey?" Larissa feigned surprise. "I was under the impression that you just snorted it straight."

"Smartass."

"Yes, my ass is smart."

"And cute. Finish your coffee, come back to bed, and I'll show you just how cute I think it is."

"Not until you tell me what's the matter."

"What are you talking about?"

"I know you, Gabriel," Larissa said. "And I know when something is bothering you. Tell me what it is."

"Nothing."

"Don't lie to me."

Asher knew she wouldn't let it go. Her love and concern for him could be stubborn sometimes. She would not relent until he talked to her about the darkness brewing inside. And while part of him wished she would just drop the issue, the other part was grateful that she insisted there be no secrets between them. He knew better than most that secrets could kill a relationship.

"It's just the usual shit," he said. "You know how it is."

The gunfire, the screams, the blood, the battles, the scars on his soul from the things he had done in order to survive...

She swirled her cup of coffee, then took a slow, deliberate sip, giving him the space, the time, to break his words free from their internal prison and talk to her.

"Sometimes," he finally said, "I just hate the job." He paused, then added, "I also hate talking about it."

"If you really don't want to talk about it," Larissa said, "then of course you don't have to. I'm not going to make you do something you don't want to do. But we've been down this road before, so you know that if you bottle things up and keep it all tucked down deep inside, they eventually find a way to come crawling back up. And when they do, it's always worse than if you had just talked about things in the first place." She reached out and put a hand on his arm. "I'm not here to judge you, Gabe. I'm your friend, your lover, your *part-ner*. I'm here to listen, to help you with whatever demons you're fighting."

Asher nodded despite the fact that she couldn't see him, but didn't say anything. He hated to burden her with the things that haunted him, but he also knew that sharing burdens was part of being with someone. He just needed to learn how to do it better.

"Talk to me, Gabe," she said, giving his arm a gentle squeeze. "Tell me the truth, whatever it is. Whatever's bothering you. I need to hear it."

"The truth is that I'm tired of the killer's life," he replied. "I want something more, something better. I've got so many ghosts that haunt my sleep, and I keep adding to the tally to keep you—to keep *us*—safe."

"Don't let it break you," Larissa said. "Whatever regrets you have, whatever ghosts, somehow you have to learn to live with them."

"The only thing that would break me is losing you."

"That's not going to happen. I'm more worried about you losing your soul in all this."

"Sometimes I'm not sure I even have one anymore."

"Of course you do. Never forget who you are, Gabriel Asher. You're a man who sacrificed everything to protect someone he loves. You put your life on the line for me, for Malakai, for Shiomi, and even for your country. They have a name for that. It's called honor."

"I killed dozens of men last night," he said. "Not sure I would call that honorable."

"The world is better off without men like that, and you know it."

A heartbeat after the words left her mouth, the house exploded around them.

The concussive force of the blast momentarily robbed Asher of his coherency. The world went dark, blackness claiming his senses for a few seconds. He struggled to stay conscious, thinking not of himself, but of Larissa. He saw her picked up and thrown into the corner of the kitchen by the blast.

He landed on his back and skidded up against the far wall, his ears ringing horribly. Smoke and debris left him half-blinded, vision compromised. He tried to call out to Larissa but choked on the smoke and dust, the breath ragged in his throat.

He shook away the dizziness and assessed his condition. No injuries that he could tell, aside from some minor cuts, scrapes, and bruises.

He quickly scrambled over to Larissa. She sprawled in a crumpled heap where the kitchen cabinets were intersected by the stove. She was alive, her eyes open, but blood blotched the left side of her face. Looked like she wasn't as lucky as he was. He saw the wound. A piece of shrapnel had grazed a shallow trench along her temple. Like any scalp injury, it bled like hell and looked worse than it actually was.

"You okay?" he asked.

She coughed through the smoke filling the air with noxious fumes. "I'm fine." She sounded calm, not panicked. This wasn't the first time violence had struck her life. "What happened?"

"Not sure, but my guess would be an RPG."

"Which means..."

"Which means we're being attacked, and there's probably a hit team inbound," Asher said. "Stay down and out of sight."

"Be careful."

Asher grabbed the dish towel off the oven handle, pressed it against her scalp wound, told her to keep pressure on it, and then hustled back into the bedroom to get his guns. Chubbs passed him in the hallway, racing to find Larissa. Asher tucked the HK45 Tactical pistol into the waistband of his sweatpants and grabbed his Franchi SPAS-12 combat shotgun. His fingers itched to get it on the triggers.

They had attacked him at his home.

Attacked *Larissa*.

Whoever they were, he was going to kill them all.

He shoved spare shells and magazines into his pants pockets and went back out into the kitchen. Larissa remained against the cabinets, Chubbs now by her side.

Through the hole in the wall caused by the grenade, he saw black-clad men swarming toward the house. They were all armed with submachine guns.

Asher raised the shotgun to his shoulder and stepped outside. Rage mixed with adrenaline to send a hot cocktail blazing through his veins. He could have hunkered down and waited for the fight to come to him, but the hell with that. If the invaders made it inside, Larissa was at risk. He could not allow that to happen. No, he would take the fight right to the bastards.

Outside, Asher immediately pivoted to the left and launched into an evasive sprint, his faux-moccasins crunching through the snow. He kept the SPAS-12 pressed to his shoulder as he ran and fired at the first target he acquired. The double-ought buckshot blasted into the assaulter's chest and blew him off his feet. One of his teammates whirled into view from behind a tree and caught Asher's second shot right in the head. The man's skull exploded like a rotten grapefruit struck by a sledgehammer. Bone, blood, and brains flew everywhere.

He rounded the corner of the house and nearly collided with another attacker. Caught off guard, the guy's eyes widened in surprise, and he tried to get his gun into play. But Asher triggered on the run and blew the man straight to hell with a point-blank buckshot blast to the upper torso.

Asher paused with his back against the house to shove fresh shells into the SPAS-12, breath pluming in the cold morning air. Shirtless, he should have been shivering, but the adrenaline kept him warm enough, injecting heat into his bloodstream. It dawned on him that so far, none of these clowns were wearing body armor. Despite the RPG and automatic weapons, this was not a professional strike team.

So who the hell had sent them?

It was impossible to take a guess, since he had so many enemies, so many people who would be happy to see him turned into maggot food.

Worry about neutralizing the threat for now. Time enough to figure out the who and the why later.

Auto-fire chewed at the corner of the house, a few feet away from where he stood. He dropped into a kneeling position, spun around the edge, and hammered another face with buckshot. The gunner went down silently—hard to make a sound with your mouth pulverized—and died with his hot blood sizzling the snow.

They were storming the house with little, if any, strategy. No tactical proficiency. Just a forward rush, like bulls charging a red cape.

No, not bulls.

Sitting ducks.

Asher swung the shotgun onto the next target and hit the gunman low, blowing apart the pelvic girdle. The man screamed as the thick bone shattered and his groin exploded into pulp. Asher didn't let him suffer. The follow-up shot took the top of the guy's head off. Everything above the eyes vanished in a red slurry.

Two more gunners appeared from the pine trees lining the riverbank. They rained twin lines of fire down on Asher's position as he kneeled in the snow. The bullets kicked up geysers of white powder as they tracked toward him. The initial salvos had missed him by a wide margin, further proof of the hit team's lack of proficiency. But they were getting closer the longer the pair of gunmen held down the triggers and burned through their magazines.

Asher ducked back around the corner of the house before they could find the range. He heard slugs pound into the front wall and chunks of shredded vinyl siding slashed into his field of vision like shrapnel. More amateur hour stupidity. With Asher out of sight, the attackers were just wasting bullets, firing at the house.

He gripped the shotgun and waited. He kept watching over his shoulder as well. If they were smart, they would come at him from front and back. He kept his head on a swivel, scanning one hundred eighty degrees every few seconds. If they synchronized perfectly, they might have a chance at taking him down. But from what he had seen so far, he doubted these assholes were capable of that level of tactical precision.

Sure enough, the guy coming in from the front showed himself first instead of waiting for his partner. Asher heard the crunch of snow under the man's boots and was ready when he came into view. The SPAS-12 roared again and sent two rapid loads of buckshot ripping through the bastard's chest. The target went down as if kicked by a horse, sternum smashed by the sledgehammer impacts. He didn't even grunt in pain. Just fell backward into the snow and died with his chest cavity exposed to the cold mountain air.

Asher spun in the opposite direction, and seconds later, the second gunner appeared, just a couple of heartbeats too late to do his partner any good. He barely settled his eyes on Asher before the shotgun blew his guts out all over the snow, and he went down with a gaping crater where his belly used to be. He proved to be a tough son of a bitch and tried to bring his gun into play even as he died, but Asher finished him off with a follow-up shot to the face. Blowing a man's eyeballs out the back of his head wasn't pretty, but it got the job done.

As the corpse twitched and spasmed in death's throes, Asher heard the sound of an engine firing up. He whipped his head around and turned his attention back to the front of the property. He spotted a man sprinting across the bridge toward an SUV waiting at the driveway's entrance. Looked like the strike team—what was left of it, anyway—was about to cut their losses and jackrabbit the hell out of there.

"Not so fast, you piece of shit." Asher growled.

The range between him and the fleeing gunman was at least eighty yards, well beyond the shotgun's effective range. Even if he managed to hit the runner with some buckshot, it would most likely sting him at best, not bring him down.

Asher ditched the SPAS-12 and drew the HK45.

He took off after the guy, firing one-handed as he ran. The pistol wasn't particularly accurate past fifty yards, but if he managed to put one or more of the 9mm bullets on target, it stood a better chance of bringing down his prey than the buckshot. He dumped half a magazine as he barreled toward the bridge, trying to nail the gunman before the gunman got to the SUV and fled the scene.

The man suddenly staggered as one of Asher's bullets struck flesh, but he didn't go down. Still on his feet but limping badly, he continued toward his waiting ride. He thrust his weapon over his shoulder and cut loose with a full-auto burst that came surprisingly close to connecting with Asher, who had to jump to the side as the slugs kicked up snow where he'd been standing a second before. Thank God for quick reflexes. Would have been embarrassing to die from a lucky burst fired by a crippled amateur.

Asher hit the ground on his shoulder and used his own momentum to roll back up onto his feet, ignoring the snow that covered him like a bad case of dandruff. He continued chasing after the wounded gunman, who was now climbing into the SUV and yelling, "Go, go, go!" The engine revved, screaming its intention to get the hell out of there.

Cursing, Asher hurled himself forward, more reckless than usual, determined not to let these bastards get away. As his feet hit the bridge, he fired three more shots on the run just as the SUV's door closed. The bullets sparked off the vehicle's bodywork.

Snowy gravel rooster-tailed from beneath the SUV's tires as the driver punched the gas pedal. Asher reached the end of the bridge in time to unload the rest of his magazine at the escaping vehicle, dumping rounds into the back tires and then into the rear window. Glass shattered, but the tires must have been run-flats, because the SUV kept on rolling.

"Dammit!"

Realizing the SUV—and its occupants—were going to make good on their getaway, Asher locked his eyes on the license plate.

ADV4615

He committed the plate to memory as he ejected the spent magazine from the HK45 and popped in a fresh one. He let the pistol hang down by his side as he turned and looked across the lawn at the smoking hole in the front of his house, the multiple corpses staining the snow. The morning sun shining down seemed in stark contrast to the blood, death, and destruction strewn everywhere. He used his free hand to brush the snow off his bare chest and shoulders.

"Gabe?" Larissa appeared, framed in the jagged crater. Her voice carried down to the bridge. "Are you okay?"

"I'm fine," he called back, returning the pistol to the waistband of his sweatpants. "I'll be there in a minute."

"Are they dead?"

"Most of them, yeah."

"What about the ones that aren't dead?"

"Gone."

"They got away?"

"Yeah."

Asher walked back and retrieved the SPAS-12. Methodically, he pulled shells from his pocket and reloaded the shotgun, not really thinking about it, his fingers simply working with muscle memory. His mind was elsewhere, wondering who the hell had the audacity to come here and attack him at home. Either somebody stupid or somebody powerful. Time to run the damn plates and find out.

Back in the house, he checked Larissa's scalp wound. Just a graze, so it had already stopped bleeding. "You okay?" he asked.

"I'm fine."

He gave her a quick hug and then grabbed his phone. "I'm calling the Church."

"Can you trust them?" she asked. "What if they had something to do with the attack?"

"They didn't."

"How can you be so sure?"

"If the kill order was back in place, the Company would have sent pros," Asher replied. "These dipshits were a bunch of amateurs."

Standing in the wreckage of his kitchen, he dialed a number and pressed the phone to his ear. Larissa stood nearby, saying nothing, letting him work.

The phone rang twice, then: "This is Wyatt."

Great. As if the day couldn't get any fucking worse.

"It's Asher. Get Vesper."

"You know, I'm support personnel too. Just tell me what you need, and I'll take care of it."

"If I wanted you to take care of it, I wouldn't ask for Vesper."

Wyatt sighed. "You know, Asher, I'm getting extremely tired of your constant disrespect. Keep it up and you may have cause to regret it."

"That a threat?"

"No, those are your specialty, not mine. Here's Vesper."

Her voice came on the line. "Hi, Gabe, it's me. What can I do for you?"

"Need you to run a plate for me."

"Wyatt could have done that, you know."

"I don't deal with that prick unless I have to."

Vesper laughed. "Okay, fine. Fire away."

Asher gave her the letter-number combination, reciting from memory.

"I take it you had a run-in with whoever owns the plates?"

Asher glanced at the destruction all around him. The house was growing colder by the minute as the winter air poured in through the hole in the wall. "Yeah, I guess you could say that."

"Give me a minute or two."

Asher heard clacking on the keyboard as Vesper started working her computer magic. She said nothing, focused on the task at hand. He stayed quiet too, not wanting to interrupt her.

While he waited, Asher looked at Larissa. She seemed to stare back at him, even though that was obviously impossible due to her blindness. He could tell she was a bit rattled by the violent ordeal they had just suffered, but she was holding it together just fine and did not appear too shaken up. Not much of a surprise, really, since this wasn't her first rodeo. She'd been married to an assassin before, and then found herself thrust by God, fate, or destiny back into Asher's orbit, so she was well acquainted with the dangers of the gunslinger lifestyle.

But it's supposed to be less dangerous now, he thought. *That was the whole point of agreeing to resurrect Black Talon—to keep her safe.*

He needed answers—who had attacked him and why—and he needed them fast.

"Got it," Vesper said on the other end of the line. "And oh my god, I hope you're sitting down, because you're not going to believe this."

"You'd be surprised what I'll believe these days," Asher replied.

"Yeah, well, I still doubt you'll see this one coming," said Vesper. "The vehicle is registered to Rene Perelli."

CHAPTER 8

ASHER TACKED some plastic sheeting over the grenade-blasted hole in the front of his house. Once he contacted Olander, she would dispatch a construction team to handle the repairs and a cleanup crew to take care of the bodies. What the cleaners did with all the corpses, Asher had never bothered to ask. His job was the killing. Disposal was somebody else's department.

He had relayed to Larissa the information Vesper had given him, then told her to pack a bag and get ready to hit the road. "No way in hell we're staying here."

"Where are we going? A safe house?"

"Not until I know for sure who I can trust."

"You think someone set you up?"

"Our location is not a matter of public record," he said. "Due to security concerns, Olander made sure this place and Malakai's down in Florida were buried deep enough that it would take some serious digging to figure out where we lived."

"So you think someone in Black Talon betrayed you, gave up our address?"

"I don't know *what* to think," he answered.

"Who would do that, and why?"

"I don't know the answer to either one of those questions. But I'm damn sure going to find out."

Less than an hour after the attack, they were packed up and on the road. They brought the bare necessities—clothes, toiletries, food—and an assortment of weapons. Asher debated calling Malakai but decided to hold off. Rene Perelli was his problem, and he would deal with it alone for now. No reason to spoil Malakai's time with Shiomi. He could always call his friend for backup later if it became necessary.

As he drove down Route 73 past the scenic Roaring Brook Falls, he wondered what had caused Perelli to stop honoring their truce. He'd had her dead to rights back in the day, pinned to the end of his pistol, and he had let her live in exchange for her promise not to come after him or the ones he loved.

Guess that deal's broken now. Should have put her down when I had the chance.

There was a time after his wife's death and before Larissa came back into his life when he would have shown her no mercy and put a bullet through her heart without hesitation. But Larissa had awakened his humanity, made him want to stop his killing ways, and had reconnected him to a softer, less-primal part of his nature. Even after Perelli's threats, after her assassination attempts on his and Larissa's lives, he had let her walk away from the end of his gun barrel.

"I don't want to kill you," he had said to her. *"I'm letting you have your life. Let this war end right here, right now."*

Now she had repaid his reclaimed conscience by

blowing apart his house and trying to execute him at his own home. Apparently, leaving him alone was just too damn much to ask. Not that he completely blamed her. After all, he *had* killed her husband while working under a freelance contract with the Giadello crime family. Sure, her husband had kicked down the dominos that led to his death by starting a turf war with the Giadellos, but justifications didn't matter much to a grieving widow. Especially when there was a young daughter left behind, an innocent who couldn't really comprehend why her daddy was gone forever.

Yeah, Asher knew better than most that sometimes tears demanded payback.

He steered the Ram Rebel 1500 Crew Cab onto I-87 and set the cruise at a conservative 70 mph, heading an hour south to the Glens Falls area, his old stomping grounds. Larissa napped with her head against the window, lulled to sleep by the motion of the truck, while Chubbs sat in the back seat and watched the mountain scenery rush by. The German shepherd's ears occasionally pricked up when he spotted something interesting, like a whitetail deer skirting the edge of a frozen pond. Snow capped the peaks on either side of the highway.

Asher paid no attention to the rugged beauty around him. His mind raced, trying to figure out a reason why they had been attacked, especially after all this time. The truce had held for well over a year, so why had Rene Perelli chosen to violate it now? He needed to talk to Olander, see if she had any insight on the matter.

He pulled off the interstate about an hour north of Albany and found a cheap chain hotel nestled in the middle of fast-food restaurants and gas stations. His stomach growled, reminding him that he was hungry, and some food was in order. He would see to that right after he called Olander. If he was hungry, no doubt Larissa and Chubbs were too.

Inside the cramped lobby of the hotel, he was greeted by a disheveled man behind the desk who reeked of cigarettes and last night's beer. The smell of burned coffee hung in the air, and there was a rack of brochures that nobody would ever read tucked against the wall next to a half-dead potted plant. Asher paid for the room with cash, gave the uncaring clerk a fake name, and then went back out to the truck, where Larissa was now awake.

"Where are we?" she asked.

"Motel. We'll hole up here while I figure things out."

He guided her to their room on the first floor and then retrieved their gear. The place was basic but clean, though it smelled like someone had gone a little too gung ho with the Pine-Sol. Still, better too much cleaning solution than grime and cockroaches.

Larissa sat down on the edge of the bed while Chubbs hopped up beside her, spun around twice, and then flopped down with his head on his paws. "Smells really clean," she said.

"Smells like a hospital," Asher replied.

"We could've been in the morgue," she said, "so I guess we shouldn't complain."

"We've got plenty to complain about," Asher said. "But this place isn't one of them. It's just a place to crash and hide out for a few."

"Should I bother unpacking?"

"We won't be staying long." He fished out his cell phone. "I need to make a call."

They were safe enough for now. They could lie low here for the day, maybe two, while he figured out where things stood and what he needed to do about it. He dialed Olander's number directly, not bothering to call the Church and have Vesper route him.

She answered on the first ring. "I've been expecting to hear from you."

"Bad news travels fast, I guess."

"I've got the big picture, but give me the details."

"I don't have any details. All I know is that Rene Perelli tried to kill me."

"You absolutely sure about that?"

"The bitch sent a kill team to my house, blew it half to shit, and tried to take me out."

"Damn." Olander sounded genuinely troubled by the information. "If that's true, then that's a real dirty move on Perelli's part."

"It's true," Asher said. "The fuckers showed up in an SUV, and I managed to get the plates. Vesper ran them, and they came back to Perelli."

"She told me."

"Something else to consider...My home address is not very easy to get."

"You think we have a leak?"

"Don't you?"

"Systems can be hacked. I don't want to jump right to the conclusion that we've got a traitor in our midst." Olander sighed. "But it's definitely a possibility. I'll grant you that."

"Anybody come to mind?"

"There's a congressman with a bug up his ass about

the program who would love to see it shut down, but he's squeamish about killing, so organizing your murder seems a bit of a stretch.

"Yeah, well, somebody gave Perelli the information."

"So what's your next move?" Olander asked.

"I think you know."

"Probably, but I'd still like to hear you say it out loud."

"I'm going after Perelli and her whole goddamned organization," Asher rasped. "I'm gonna burn it to the ground and spit on the ashes."

"I'm not convinced that's the best course of action right now."

"The bitch tried to kill me. Worse, she tried to kill Larissa. You think I'm just going to stand by and do nothing?"

"What I think," said Olander, "is that you need to slow down, take a breath, and think about this before you start setting the world on fire."

Asher was in no mood to put the brakes on. "Do I need to remind you about the terms of our agreement?"

"Our arrangement has multiple terms attached to it," Olander replied. "Which one are you referring to?"

"The one that says I get to go after any target that I deem a threat."

"I did agree to that, yes."

"The bitch tried to kill us in our own house," Asher growled. "Pretty sure that counts as a threat. So don't dick me around and let me get rolling on some payback."

Olander took a deep breath, sighed into the phone, and said, "Sorry, but I'm going to have to say no."

Anger cut through him like a knife, cold and sharp. "Did you just tell me no?"

"That's exactly what I told you. Need me to repeat it? Need to hear the words 'direct order' to make it official?"

Asher felt like punching something. He considered putting his fist through the wall, but then thought better of it. Instead, he gritted his teeth so hard he thought the enamel would shatter. "You really think it's wise to tell me no right now?"

"I have my reasons."

"Care to show your cards?"

"Not right now."

"Fine. You don't want to honor our deal, I've got a new deal for you. I'm fucking done. You hear me? You renege on your promise, then I walk away from you, from Black Talon, from everything."

"And I can reinstate the kill order against you and Malakai. You'll have headhunters dogging you in every corner of the globe."

"And I'll send them back to you in body bags."

"So that's where we're at?" Olander sounded like she couldn't believe it had come to this.

"Just laying out the facts for you. If you give me a reason to walk, then I will."

Asher knew pushing her this hard was a risk, but it was one he was willing to take. She had made promises when he returned to the killing business, and he expected her to keep them. If she thought dangling a guillotine over his neck would keep him compliant, she was sorely mistaken. He wasn't asking permission to target Rene Perelli. He was simply telling her what he was going to do.

Whether the senator liked it or not did not factor into his decision.

It was his call, and he had made it.

"Can I propose a different strategy?" Olander asked.

"Like what?"

"Stand down for twenty-four hours."

"What happens in twenty-four hours?"

"It gives me time to make some calls, put out some feelers. Meet me at the Floyd Bennett Memorial Airport tomorrow morning, and I'll explain everything. You know where that is, right?"

"Yeah, I know it."

"I know you're angry," said Olander, "but I assure you, it will be in your best interest."

What the hell kind of game is she playing at? Asher longed for the old days when he was on his own, trusting nobody but himself. In some ways, *many* ways, life had been easier back then. Having friends, lovers, and handlers left you vulnerable. Not that he regretted his friendship with Malakai or his romance with Larissa, but there was no denying that without them, his existence had been a whole lot simpler.

"Fine," he replied. "But I'm bringing Malakai with me. If this is some kind of setup, if I think I'm getting burned, then we go into war mode, and all bets are off. Understand?"

"So now you don't trust me?"

"My house has a big fucking hole in it, there are more dead guys on my lawn than dogshit, and I'm on the run, so I'm a little short on trust right now."

"Well, I can tell you this much," Olander said. "If

there's another hit, I guarantee Rene Perelli won't be behind it."

"How can you be so sure? What aren't you telling me?"

"Like I said, I'll explain everything in the morning. Just don't do anything stupid before then."

"You better have some answers for me tomorrow."

"I will. You have my word." Olander ended the call.

Asher tossed the phone on the nightstand. They would hunker down here at the hotel for the day, get a good night's sleep, and then see what tomorrow brought. If he didn't like the answers Olander provided —or she failed to provide them at all—then he would go on the warpath. Olander might think she wore the pants and held his leash, but she would find out that he called no man—or woman—master. He had gone to guns with his employers before and walked away intact, nothing but scorched earth behind him. He would do it again if it came down to that.

He explained everything to Larissa. She listened quietly, intently, asking questions here and there. She insisted on going with him unless he called Malakai. Since he didn't know what he would be walking into tomorrow, and he wanted her out of harm's way, he promised to phone his friend. Only then did she agree to stay in the motel with Chubbs while he went to the airport to meet Olander. The dog would give his life defending her, and Asher would leave her a gun as well. He himself would be armed up with his HK45 pistol, extra magazines, and his KA-BAR knife. Hell, he might even throw on some Kevlar, just in case.

He wanted to trust Olander, but trust was in short supply right now.

But more than anything, he just wanted the truth.

CHAPTER 9

MALAKAI HATED FIGHTING WITH SHIOMI.

Their relationship was strong, their love having been forged in the fires of hardship and betrayal, so thankfully, their disagreements were infrequent. But no relationship was immune to the occasional downturn. They kept it civil—no shouting or hostile words—but Malakai still didn't like it. And the truth was, these days, they pretty much only fought about one topic.

Kids.

"Just tell me why."

"I've told you why," Malakai replied. "Hundreds of times. Hell, maybe thousands."

"All you've really done is give me reasons why you think we shouldn't without even considering my reasons for why we should."

"My reasons are good. They make sense."

"You're saying mine aren't?" Shiomi asked, a challenge in her voice.

Malakai didn't answer. Even in disagreements, he tried his best not to insult or ignore her feelings. She had suffered enough hurt in her life—her prosthetic leg alone was proof of that—and he had no desire to add to it. He respected that she wanted children, or at least wanted to consider the possibility of starting a family, but he couldn't change how he felt. Still, if it was important to her, he couldn't just dismiss it, despite his misgivings on the matter.

"No," he said. "That's not what I'm saying."

"That's what it sounded like."

"Guess I should have been clearer, then."

"That would be helpful."

They were standing in the living room of their house in Homosassa Springs, Florida. A large saltwater aquarium nestled against the wall, and Malakai turned to face it, seeking a momentary respite from the argument. The aquarium was testimony to his ability to change, to adapt, to overcome, even the things he feared the most.

He had suffered from ichthyophobia, fear of fish, from a young age due to a red-bellied piranha severing his pinkie. It still surfaced at times, but for the most part, he had brought it under control. He had installed the aquarium in their house as a reminder that he was stronger than his fears.

Maybe he was stronger than his fear of bringing a child into his violent, uncertain life. Or his fear that he would be a horrible father, just like his father before him.

He watched the colorful fish dart leisurely through the large tank, unconcerned—perhaps even unaware—that they were trapped in a glass cage. Alive but not free. And while he would never say it out loud, he secretly hoped that he would never feel trapped or caged in by the life Shiomi wanted for him.

For *them*.

Without warning, she changed the subject, as if she had already tired of the fight. "I had the nightmare again last night."

"I thought I heard you cry out once."

"It's getting worse, Malakai. I keep seeing his face every time I close my eyes. I'm not sure how much longer I can take it."

He turned away from the aquarium and faced her again.

"He's always there," she continued, brushing a wayward strand of hair out of her eyes. "Watching me, just like he used to." She shuddered involuntarily, her internal torment given physical manifestation.

The *he* she was referring to was her former pimp, the lowlife scumbag who worked for the Syndicate running the hookers in the Miami area. Shiomi had managed to escape his clutches, but he still haunted her, a demon from her horrible, abusive past.

I should have made him a ghost when I had the chance, Malakai thought.

"I just want to stop seeing him," she said. "I want him out of my head."

Malakai understood completely. She had suffered horribly at the cruel hands of the Syndicate, and while her father had masterminded the abuse, the pimp had facilitated it. And while her father had paid the ultimate price, killed by Malakai, the pimp remained alive and unpunished for his sins.

What he had done to her, forcing her to sell her body on the street, often to the roughest of clients, deserved a reckoning. Only by some inner strength had she avoided being destroyed by the endless degradation. A lesser woman would have broken, resorted to drugs or suicide. But Shiomi had refused to let her hell consume her. And when the opportunity came to escape that hell, with Malakai's help, she seized it.

But the scars remained.

"I just can't get rid of him," she said. "Just when I think he's gone, he comes back, in my thoughts, my dreams."

Malakai stepped over, took her hand, and gazed solemnly into her dark, exotic eyes. "I can make sure he's gone for good."

"Even if you kill him, he'll still be in my head."

"I can't fix that, but I can make sure your head is the only place he exists, not walking around wasting God's good air, and maybe that will help you heal." He pulled her close, bringing her hands to his chest. "Let me find him. Let me hunt him down and finish him off for what he did to you."

Tears brimmed in Shiomi's eyes, tears created from both the memories of her past and the knowledge of just how much he loved her. Malakai wanted nothing more than to vanquish whatever was behind those tears, the pain she sometimes struggled to talk about, the wounds that would never be fully healed, no matter how much time passed.

"I can't ask you to do that," she said. "He's my problem, not yours."

"Your problems *are* my problems," Malakai replied. "Besides, he's a scumbag that deserves to be put down. I'd happily do it for you."

"I know you would."

Outside the window, the light of day began to yield to the evening shadows. Malakai pulled Shiomi close, and she leaned her head against his chest as his arms encircled her shoulders protectively. He whispered to her that everything was going to be all right.

They stayed that way, content in their closeness, until his cell phone rang.

"I can ignore it," he said.

"In your line of work, you're never really off the clock," Shiomi said. "You should at least check and see who it is."

"Whoever it is, they're not more important than you."

She smiled up at him. "How romantic of you. Now answer the damn phone."

He broke their embrace and pulled the phone out of his pocket, glancing at the caller ID. "It's Gabe."

"Now you really have to answer it," she said.

Malakai tapped the screen to accept the call. "Hey, man. What's up?"

"We have a problem," Asher said without preamble.

Shiomi wandered over to watch the aquarium as Malakai asked, "What kind of problem?"

"Rene Perelli muscled her way into my backyard this morning."

"I thought you two had an understanding."

"So did I. Until she blew a fucking hole in the side of my house and sent in a kill team to take us out."

"You okay?"

"I'm still breathing. They're not."

"Dead assholes are my favorite kind. How's Larissa?"

"A little shaken up, but she's tough."

"That's for damn sure."

"I guess you know why I'm calling," Asher said.

"You don't even have to ask."

"I'm asking, anyway. This isn't your fight."

"You're my friend. Your fight is my fight."

"Seriously, no hard feelings if you sit this one out."

Malakai glanced at Shiomi. She turned away from the aquarium and headed toward the bedroom, giving him a sultry smile as she sauntered by. Her hand reached out and brushed her fingers across his chest as she glided past, her eyes full of promise. His body responded to her touch, his need to be with her more like an ache down in his soul. It was all he could do not to hang up the phone and drag her to bed.

But business first. Pleasure could wait a few more minutes. There were enemies that needed to be dealt with, and no way in hell was he letting Asher fight those enemies alone.

"Tell me where and when to meet you," he said.

"I'm meeting Olander at the airport in Glens Falls tomorrow morning. She claims she can shed some light on the subject."

"I'll be there."

"You sure?"

Malakai said, "Stop acting like you wouldn't do the same for me and shut up about it."

"Fair enough. Thanks."

"See you tomorrow."

They ended the call, and Malakai went into the bedroom, where he found Shiomi curled up in the middle of the bed, her dark hair fanned out across the pillow, her clothes on the floor. She wore a nightgown that left absolutely nothing to the imagination.

"You're leaving again," she said. It wasn't a question.

He discarded his own clothing, stretched out on the bed beside her, and kissed her deeply. When they came up for air, he grazed her cheek with the back of his hand and said, "Not until later tonight."

"That's when Gabe needs you?"

"Yeah. I need to be in New York by morning."

She pulled him to her, her voice husky as she whispered, "Well, I need you right now."

They spent the next few hours in slow, passionate lovemaking. The earlier fight and fears were forgotten as their hearts and bodies found each other all over again. By morning, he would be standing by Asher's side, but tonight, he was all hers.

There would always be plenty of people for him to kill, but there was only one woman for him to love. In a world of darkness, she was the light he clung to.

After, with the sweat cooling on their skin, they slept, content in each other's arms. Tomorrow might bring more blood and savagery, but tonight, there was only love and the salvation it could bring.

Too bad it couldn't last forever.

CHAPTER 10

LATER THAT NIGHT—OR very early the next morning, depending on your viewpoint—Shiomi drove Malakai to the airport. Their parting kiss was quick but passionate, and she was grateful their relationship had not devolved to the point of perfunctory goodbye pecks.

As always, neither he nor she knew how long he would be gone. A day, a few days, a week? That was up to the fickle gods of war. It was one of the mysteries of his job, of their life together. All she knew was that Rene Perelli had attacked Asher and Larissa, and now the threat needed to be dealt with. There was no way Malakai could leave his friend hanging, and Shiomi did not expect him to.

Despite their arguments about having children, she did not want to change him. He was an assassin, a warrior, a man willing and capable of resorting to violence at a moment's notice. She had fallen in love with a gunslinger, not a priest. But he was a gunslinger with a heart, and because he was that kind of man, he had pulled her out of the cesspool of dirty hotel rooms and dirtier men that he had found her in. With love and fury, he had laid waste to anyone who stood in the way of her freedom.

But one score remained unsettled.

With Malakai off helping Asher, she had an opportunity to help herself. To hammer another nail in the coffin of her past and let another wound start to heal.

Time to drive down to Miami and pay a visit to Nick Caesar, the albino scarecrow of a man who also happened to be her ex-pimp. Her father—now dead and gone at Malakai's hand, or rather, grenade—might have given the order for his daughter to be trafficked, but Caesar was the one who actually farmed her out.

He was nothing more than a degenerate cockroach clinging parasitically to the ass end of the Syndicate empire. He was a scumbag living in a scummy apartment dealing in a scummy business.

She knew where his apartment was. In all the years she'd worked for him, he'd never moved once. She intended to drive down, knock on his door, and shoot him in the face. Probably more than once. Malakai didn't even need to know what happened. It wasn't that she was keeping secrets from him. This was just something she needed to do for herself.

She jumped on the turnpike and headed south. The Florida sun beat down through the windshield, but the car's air conditioner kept the heat at bay. But it couldn't cool the rage simmering in her veins. She'd suffered years of pain at the hands of Nick Caesar, and now she would make him pay. Maybe if she killed the beast, slayed her demon, the nightmares would cease.

She briefly wondered if he would recognize her when she showed up at his door and shoved a gun in his face. Then she stopped wondering, because, of course, he would. She had not just been some nameless face in the sea of working girls. She had been the daughter of Tanaka, the head of the Syndicate's East Coast operations. Not somebody you forgot quickly.

Five hours later, she was standing outside the door to his studio apartment. She heard multiple voices inside, though the exact conversation was drowned out by the rock music blasting away with the bass cranked high enough to shake the walls. It sounded like some old school '80s heavy metal, maybe Judas Priest or Iron Maiden. God knew she was no expert on the genre. Whatever it was, it was so loud that nobody heard her when she knocked.

No need to be timid, she told herself. *You came here to kill a man, so knock on that damn door like you mean it.*

She knocked again, this time more forcefully.

The music volume went down a decibel or two, and a male's voice called out, "Hey, is there somebody at the door?"

"Why?" another voice asked. "You hear something?"

"Thought I heard a knock."

"Then go check it out, dumbass."

"Why don't *you* check it out, fucknuts?"

"Can't you see I'm a little busy here?"

"You ain't doing shit. She's doing all the work."

"Just answer the goddamned door already."

Shiomi waited patiently. Neither of the voices belonged to Nick Caesar, but that didn't mean he wasn't there. Her right hand delved inside her purse, fingers wrapped around the suppressed 9mm Glock 17 pistol. No nervous sweat slickened her skin. She felt cool, calm, and collected, ready to waste the monster that had sold her body for so many years. How many times had she been summoned to this very apartment and forced to service some client on the satin sheets of Caesar's heart-shaped waterbed? Not Caesar, of course. He was gay and preferred love dolls to actual people, but he had plenty of friends who had been all too happy to abuse her.

Usually, she tried her best to repress the unpleasant memories. But not today. No, today those memories fueled her anger, her shame, laid wide open the wounds of the past so she could avenge the sins committed against her.

Thinking about all she had suffered before Malakai rescued her—before they had rescued *each other*—would make it easy to pull the trigger when the moment came. She might not be able to bring the Syndicate's criminal empire down, but she could definitely reduce the number of players by one.

Nick Caesar didn't know it yet, but he had trafficked his last girl.

Unless he could traffic them in hell.

She used her left hand to knock again, practically beating on the door.

"Hold your fucking horses!"

She heard footsteps approaching, and a moment later the door yanked open and a young man stood in the opening wearing nothing but black silk boxers, his hairy chest lathered with sweat. Late twenties, maybe early thirties, his build rangy and lean. Cocaine speckled the tip of his nose, and his semi-erection poked through the hole in his shorts.

"Well, hello there, honey." He looked Shiomi up and down, top to bottom, clearly stripping her with his eyes. Apparently, he liked what he saw because his semi-erection lost the semi part. "You must be our ten o'clock."

Shiomi didn't bother correcting him. Let him think whatever he wanted. She peered past the sweaty, coked-up pervert and saw two girls in the room, one blonde, one brunette. They were both naked, young, skinny, and big-breasted with bony legs. The blonde leaned forward to snort a line of powder, her hand shaking badly. The brunette was busy on her knees in front of the other man in the room. There was no way on God's green earth that either girl was of legal age.

Shiomi felt the acid burn of bile in the back of her throat. She almost whipped out the Glock and gunned down both men right then and there. But she managed to leash her rage. She had come here for Nick Caesar, and she didn't see him in the room.

She brushed past the man and strutted in like she owned the place, acting like a sophisticated call girl, not some gutter-trash hooker. Once inside the apartment, she scanned all directions. No sign of Caesar. But the bathroom door was closed.

As if to confirm her suspicions, the man who had greeted her at the front door yelled, "Yo, Nick, new girl just showed up, and she's prime-ass, smoking hot!"

Shiomi felt like she had just received a shot of adrenaline straight to the heart.

The bastard was here. In the bathroom for now, but he wouldn't stay there forever.

Right hand still hidden in her purse, she gripped the Glock tighter. It was almost go-time.

The place was a disaster zone, empty beer bottles strewn everywhere, fast-food containers spread haphazardly across the table and counter, Chinese noodles dangling over the sides like disemboweled intestines. The waterbed's sheets were rumpled and stained, a half-deflated love doll draped across the pillows. The whole place reeked of spilled booze, spoiled food, cheap perfume, cigarette smoke, and stale sex. The commingled stenches hung in the air like a pervasive fog.

The two girls barely glanced up. They just kept snorting and sucking.

The sweaty man didn't bother to introduce himself. He just sauntered over to the coke-snorting hooker and joined her in doing a line. Then he sighed, sank back on the couch, and snapped his fingers at Shiomi.

"Get on with it, sweet thang. Time to earn your keep. That ass ain't gonna shake itself. Get to work and show daddy a good time."

She knew she needed to play along until Caesar came out of the bathroom. She hadn't planned for this, but she had been with Malakai long enough to know that improvisation was often the key to survival. She could just stand here and do nothing, which would make them angry and suspicious, or she could play along and put them at ease until Caesar showed up.

"C'mon, bitch!" the other guy snapped, the brunette's head still bobbing in his lap. "Dance or something, for god's sake! I ain't never seen a girl with a fake leg dance. You do know how to dance, right?" He grabbed a fistful of the girl's hair and forced her to go deeper and faster, ignoring the panicked choking noises coming from her throat.

Caesar's not the only one getting a bullet tonight,

Shiomi silently vowed. Aloud, she said, "I know the *shi no odori*." She highly doubted the man knew Japanese and didn't bother to tell him that *shi no odori* meant "dance of death."

"I don't give a crap what you call it." The sweaty guy spoke this time. "Just start dancing your way out of them clothes you're wearing." He sniffed hard, inhaling the few flakes of white dust stuck to the edges of his flared nostrils. Then he started fondling the blonde, who finally looked up at Shiomi. The haunted misery in the young girl's eyes was something Shiomi had seen in the mirror far too many times, for far too long.

Stalling, she glanced at the bathroom door. *Get out here, you piece of shit.*

Time to make a decision. She was either going to have to start the gunplay early or start acting like the hooker the two men believed her to be.

You're here to kill Caesar, she reminded herself. *Do whatever it takes.*

She put thought to action, swaying her hips to the rock 'n' roll rhythms still playing softly from the stereo, her hand still inside her purse. She looked sweaty guy right in the eye and licked her lips seductively, playing the part. She had done this before and knew what the men in the room expected.

"Oh, yeah, baby girl, that's good. That's *real* good."

As she danced, Shiomi kept glancing at the bathroom door. Something deep inside her quivered with primal anticipation of the violence to come.

The sweaty man's erection was in the process of reappearing and expressing his rigid approval of her seductive moves. He leaned forward and buried his nose in another line of coke, inhaling with so much force it sounded like a jet turbine engine.

The bathroom door opened. Not even the unclicking of the lock to warn her. One moment it was closed, the next second it was wide open, and Nick Caesar stood in the doorway wearing his patented purple bikini briefs, white bunny slippers, and green feather boa. His skin glowed so palely that he damn near looked albino.

Shiomi reacted swiftly. Less than three seconds after Caesar made his sudden appearance, the pistol was out and pointed right at him. She saw his gaze go from the Glock to her face, and recognition instantly flared in his eyes.

"Shioooooomi," he said, dragging out the vowel in that crooning singsong way of his that she hated so much. There was no fear in his voice, even though he was staring down the barrel of a gun, and she hated that too.

She changed his tune by shooting him in the left knee.

The blonde and brunette both gasped as bone shattered, and Caesar went down howling in high-pitched pain. The sweaty man thrust his hands as high as they would go, as if he were reaching for the ceiling, wanting to make it clear that he was no threat.

But he was a threat. A threat to the girls in this room.

Shiomi shot him between the eyes and blew the back of his head apart like a rotten melon. It was better than the raping son of a bitch deserved.

The other guy dragged the brunette off her knees and tried to use her as a shield, like a yellow-bellied coward, but he was too slow. Shiomi's next shot tore into his throat and clipped the top of his spinal column on the way out. He dropped to the floor, dead before he could drown in his own blood.

"You crazy bitch!" Caesar screeched. He had managed to get back on his feet, leaning against the bathroom doorjamb. "You goddamned little whore!"

Shiomi looked at the two girls. "Get out," she said. "Forget my face. Forget I was ever here. Start your lives over and forget this place ever existed."

They didn't need to be told twice. They grabbed their clothes, scrambled past her, and fled out the door. The sound of their footsteps receded as they disappeared down the hall.

She was alone with the man who had put her through hell.

"Remember me, Nick?"

"I never forget a traitorous slut."

"You should probably watch your mouth. You'll live longer."

"An extra thirty seconds? You're gonna kill me anyway, so screw you."

"You deserve what you got coming."

"Maybe, but not from a used up, piece of trash bitch like you."

Shiomi was a little surprised. Caesar boasted a harder edge than when she had been under his thumb. The old Nick would have slithered and whined and begged when facing a gun, but now he just seemed to accept his fate. Like he was ready to look the Reaper in the eye and spit in his bony face. Hell, maybe he had always known this day would eventually come.

Shiomi smiled coldly. "Someone like me is exactly who should kill you, Nick."

"Never thought you would come back." Caesar giggled through his pain-clenched teeth, sounding like his old self for a moment. "Didn't think you were that stupid."

"You're not the first person to underestimate me. Just ask my father."

"Honey, you ain't nothing without that mad dog Malakai backing you."

"Pretty sure it wasn't Malakai who put a bullet in your knee a minute ago."

"So that's why you're here?" Caesar asked. "To make me pay for the sins of my past, extract your pound of flesh?"

"Exactly."

"Then get it on with it."

"You in a hurry to die?"

"Comes with the territory, sweetheart. Occupational risk. So just go on and get it over with."

Shiomi's finger trembled on the trigger. She wanted to pull it, wanted to end his life...but now that the moment had arrived, she was having trouble following through. She loved Malakai, loved him with every fiber of her heart and soul, but she wasn't like him. She wasn't a trained killer.

Pull it together, girl, she chided herself. *This is what you came here for. Don't back down now.*

Standing there, looking at the man who had caused her so much pain, so much misery, she struggled to summon the strength to pull the trigger. He had left scars on her soul, but killing him would leave another scar, this one far fresher and perhaps even harder to live with.

Then again, she had already killed the other two men in the apartment. In for a dime, in for a dollar, right?

What the hell is wrong with me? Shoot the bastard, for god's sake!

Her trembling finger refused to budge.

Instead, she heard herself saying, "Give me a reason. Give me a reason why I shouldn't put a bullet in your brain."

"All I do is run girls."

"You're not doing yourself any favors, Nick."

He stared at her with something very close to defiance. "It's not like I'm selling bombs to terrorists. Killing people isn't my cup of tea. Granted, I'm not saying my girls have a great life, but that's the nature of the game, and I'm hardly the worst pimp out there."

"So you're saying you're a piece of shit, but because there are worse pieces of shit out there, I should let you off the hook."

"I run hookers," Caesar said. "All I do is offer a service in a profession that is as old as time itself. I don't think I deserve to die for that." A shudder of pain ran through him, and he winced, clutching at his shattered knee gingerly, the bone shards pricking his palm like needles.

Shiomi couldn't even keep track of all the emotions burning through her. But one emotion she knew she wasn't feeling was sympathy. Yes, she was having a hard time pulling the trigger. But that was because she wasn't a killer, not because she felt Caesar deserved to live. Quite the opposite, in fact.

"Don't kill me," he said. "Please. I know I've done some bad shit, but..." His voice trailed off, leaving the rest unspoken.

"Bad shit? Is that what you call it?" The memories sizzled her brain like electrical shocks. The beatings she had endured at his hands, the money he had skimmed from her cut, the abuse of her friends he had forced her to watch, the times he had thrown her to the wolves to be raped by his buddies. Oh, yes, she had definitely suffered some "bad shit" at his hands.

But did that "bad shit" deserve a death sentence?

Hell yeah, it did.

The trigger felt hot to the touch, begging to be pulled.

"I just run girls," Caesar repeated.

It was the wrong thing to say.

"You don't just run girls," Shiomi snapped. "You take their lives from them. You destroy their souls. And for that, you deserve to die."

"That's for God to decide," said Caesar.

"God took the day off," she replied. "I'm filling in."

No more hesitation.

She killed him right then and there.

Phytt-phytt.

The suppressor quieted the sound of the shots as she double-tapped him in the chest, slightly left of center. The double impacts sent him staggering backward into the bathroom as blood spurted from the pair of holes in his heart. The back of his legs hit the edge of the tub, and he fell inside, somehow managing to pull the shower curtain down over him like a burial shroud as he died. Shiomi heard his final breath exhaled in a long, drawn-out groan.

Shiomi stared at his feet sticking out from beneath the tangled curtain, one of them twitching in a death spasm. Part of her felt like smiling—he was finally dead! —but another part recoiled at what she had done. She wondered if this was how Malakai felt when he assassinated the monsters and scumbags that plagued the world. She asked him about it from time to time, and he always claimed that he took no pleasure in the killing, but neither did it keep him up at night. It was just a job, nothing more. He had confided in her that Asher struggled with it more than he did.

Right now, she understood how Asher felt.

But it was done, and all she could do now was learn to live with it.

She walked out of the apartment and closed the door behind her, sealing the blood and death inside. The adrenaline spike was depleting fast, and she felt the shakes coming.

Back in the car, the revelation struck her again.

She had just killed three men. She was a murderer.

Sure, all three of those sick bastards deserved what they got, but that didn't change the fact that she had murdered them in cold blood.

Her heart pounded, and she suddenly found it hard to breathe.

How does he do it? She wondered. *How does Malakai live with all the people he's killed?*

But perhaps a bigger question was, how did she live with *herself* knowing she was in love with a killer?

She knew she needed to stop thinking, to stomp out all these dark thoughts while they were still just embers, before they could erupt into an inferno that consumed her mind and scorched her sanity. But it was easier said than done, and for at least a few moments, they served to take her mind off what she had just done, the blood she had just spilled in the name of vengeance or punishment or payback or whatever the hell you wanted to call it.

She loved Malakai with everything she had and knew that he loved her back. Despite what he did for a living, he was not heartless, even if the violence had hardened his soul. Despite his tragic upbringing, despite his years on the killing fields, he was still a good man. Hell, they had met because he was a Good Samaritan and saved her from being beaten by a customer. A more ruthless, coldhearted assassin would have just walked away and left her to her fate.

He loved her, and he had killed for her. Killed to set her free from the Syndicate's chains. Now that she knew how that felt herself, she wondered about the toll that might take on him.

Ever since putting a bullet in his father's brain at sixteen to end the abuse, Malakai had lived by the gun. A lifetime spent in solitude, surrounded by death, an endless cycle of bullets and carnage that had remained unbroken for him until she came into his life and gave him something else to live for.

Even now, the only reason he stayed in the assassination game was to keep the kill order off their heads, to keep the proverbial guillotine from dropping on their necks. Now, as before, he killed to keep her safe.

But someday, some*how*, they needed to figure out how to walk away from it all. For now, he bore the burden of death well, but who could say that it wouldn't eventually twist his soul into a hardened, gnarled knot? She didn't want to stay in the killing game long enough to see him turn into a different person. Let him ride with the Reaper too long and one day she might not recognize the man he had become. The man she had fallen in love with could end up forever lost in a world of gun smoke and shadows.

It was a path she never wanted to go down.

She looked at herself in the rearview mirror and whispered a vow into the silence. "I will not let that happen."

CHAPTER 11

THE FLOYD BENNETT Memorial Airport was quiet when Asher arrived. As a small, county-owned regional airport, it mainly serviced recreational pilots and business jets. Other than the annual Adirondack Balloon Festival every September, the place was rarely busy.

Asher sat at a corner table in the small café located inside the main building and nursed a cup of coffee. Through the floor-to-ceiling window, he had a wide view of the runway. With his back to the wall, he had a direct line of vision to the front door. He had already identified that there was a secondary exit through the kitchen and out a back door in case this meeting went hot.

He wore jeans with the HK45 pistol tucked into an IWB holster, a black sweatshirt concealing the sidearm. Spare ammo rode in a dual-magazine pouch at the small of his back, and there was a Gerber Back Up dagger tucked into a boot sheath. The Franchi SPAS-12 was out in the truck.

Malakai showed up a few minutes later, coming

through the café's main entrance, and slid into a seat at the table. He wore black jeans, a red flannel shirt, and a medium-weight jacket that Asher knew concealed an FNX-45 pistol, spare magazines, and probably a KA-BAR combat knife. He greeted Asher with a short nod and ordered a coffee when the waitress approached.

"Thanks for coming," Asher said. "Larissa insisted I not handle this alone."

"You need backup, I'll always be there," Malakai said. "You know that."

"I do know that, and I appreciate it. Friends you can trust are hard to find. They're usually trying to fuck you over instead." He couldn't help but think of Silas, his childhood best friend who ended up sleeping with his wife. He had died by Asher's hand on a rain swept road not too far from here. The bullet had been a mercy bullet, but whether or not it had also been a bullet of forgiveness, not even Asher was sure.

Ten minutes later, they watched Senator Olander's private jet touch down and taxi over to the tie-down area. Less than five minutes after that, she entered the café. She walked over to their table, her short-heeled shoes clacking sharply on the floor tile, but didn't sit down.

"Gentlemen," she greeted.

Asher wasn't in the mood for pleasantries. He got right down to business. "What's the plan?"

"We're taking a short road trip."

Asher's eyes narrowed. "How short? I'm not leaving Larissa alone while I go gallivanting across the countryside."

"We'll be at our destination in less than thirty minutes." Olander turned and marched out of the café.

Asher tossed some cash on the table to cover the coffee, and the two assassins followed her out.

"Care to tell us where we're going?" Malakai asked once they had caught up to her outside in the parking lot.

Olander either didn't hear the question or chose to ignore it. "Who's driving?"

"I've got a rental," Malakai said. "Not much bigger than a matchbox, but we should all fit."

"We can take my truck," Asher said.

They piled into the Ram Rebel, Malakai riding shotgun—literally, because the Franchi SPAS-12 was tucked under the seat—while the senator slid into the back.

"Take a right out of the airport," she said.

Asher followed her directions and then said, "You need to tell me where we're going right now."

"We're going where the answers are," Olander replied. "That's what you wanted, right? Answers?"

"Stop being so goddamned cryptic and just tell us what the hell is going on," Malakai growled.

Asher glanced over at Malakai. "If she doesn't start talking, shoot her in the leg."

"Copy that. I'm not a big believer in torture as an interrogation technique, but in this case, I'll make an exception."

"Stop being so dramatic, boys." Olander folded her arms across her chest and sighed. "We're going to the Perelli estate."

"The hell we are," Asher snapped.

"Why the fuck would we do that?" Malakai asked at the same time.

Olander replied, "You want answers? That's where they are."

"Answers? You mean a setup." Asher shot her a hard glance in the rearview mirror before returning his eyes to the road.

"This partnership doesn't work without at least a modicum of trust, gentlemen."

"Sorry," Malakai said. "The attack on his house means we're not feeling very trusting these days."

"We will figure out the parties responsible for that attack," Olander replied. "But I can assure you that neither I nor Rene Perelli had anything to do with it."

"I'd like to know how you're so sure," Asher said.

"Go to the Perelli estate, and I'll tell you everything. No secrets."

"No secrets." Malakai snorted derisively. "No way we're buying that bullshit."

Asher made a decision. "We'll go there, but the first hint that we're riding into an ambush, I'll make sure you get the first bullet." He looked at her in the rearview again. "Still want to go?"

Olander nodded. "I'm willing to put my money where my mouth is. If we arrive at the Perellis and you're attacked, you have my permission to shoot me."

"Wasn't asking permission," Asher rasped.

"Oh, really? I thought you didn't kill innocents. Isn't that part of your little prayer?"

"If we're attacked, it means you're not innocent."

They all lapsed into silence as Asher headed east out of Queensbury and picked up Route 196 in Hudson Falls, which would give them a straight shot into the farming community of Hartford, where the Perelli estate perched on top of Rowe Hill overlooking the town. The area was Asher's old stomping grounds, the place where he had grown up.

As they always did when he visited here, the memories flooded his mind.

The section of road—the Adamsville Flats, the locals called it—where he had killed Silas. The fields where he had ridden horses as a kid. The cemetery where his wife was buried. He felt a pang of guilt that he didn't visit her grave more often. Yes, she had cheated on him with Silas, but he had still loved her, and she certainly didn't deserve to be murdered by a madman. He had avenged her death, but still deeply regretted not being home to stop Colonel Macklin from killing her.

So many memories. So many ghosts. He drove a little faster, but there was no way to outrun them all. He wasn't even sure he wanted to. All those ghosts were part of who he was. He no longer believed in living in the past, but he didn't believe you should forget it, either.

His jaw tightened. He saw Olander in the rearview mirror, studying him, a look of almost concern on her face. He locked eyes with her for a moment.

"What?" he growled.

"You just suddenly looked very serious," the senator said. "Care to tell me what you're thinking about?"

"Do I look like I need a therapist?"

"You really do not want me to answer that," Olander replied. "Besides, don't you already have one? Jack Daniels, I believe the name is."

"Been a long time since I paid Jack a visit," Asher said.

"Glad to hear it."

Malakai glanced over at his friend. "You know you can just tell her to fuck off, right?"

Asher just shrugged, letting him know that Olander's opinion was irrelevant. He was more concerned about what they would encounter at Rene Perelli's place. He was seriously considering going scorched earth, wasting everyone there. They had attacked him, attacked *Larissa,* and he could not let that stand. If he walked away from this meeting with Rene Perelli still breathing, if he let her live yet again, she could just send another kill team after him.

But, of course, that was his life. He had far more enemies than friends. It would always be that way, unless he figured out a way to extract himself from the tangles of government-sanctioned assassination. God knew Larissa deserved a better life than the one he was giving her, forever trapped in a cycle of blood and bullets.

It needs to end, he thought. *Somehow, someday, I need to find a way out.*

The dark thoughts blackened his mind until he pulled up to the entrance of the Perelli estate. Raw in his self-honesty, Asher knew he let himself get dragged down into the gloom too often—a morose motherfucker Malakai had once called him—and he needed to shake it off and focus on the task at hand.

They were about to walk into the lion's den.

CHAPTER 12

INSIDE THE PERELLI HOUSE, Asher stayed quiet, but his eyes were in constant motion, scanning for threats. He kept his hand close to his HK45. Beside him, Malakai did the same. This was enemy turf. Asher considered going back to the truck and getting the shotgun.

"I don't want to die in this bitch's house," Malakai said quietly from the corner of his mouth.

"Just stay frosty," Asher replied. "Nobody's dying today." He paused. "Well, except maybe Rene Perelli."

"Hell yeah and amen."

"You're here for answers," Olander reminded them. "Not one of your killing sprees."

The senator led the way, walking through the house with strange familiarity, like it was her own.

She's been here before, Asher realized. The thought triggered his internal warning system, and the hairs on the back of his neck stood up. *Something is off. This scenario is all wrong.*

He heard the pattering of footsteps behind them,

someone light on their feet. He spun around with his hand reaching for the HK45.

A little girl, no older than eight, stood there staring at him, holding a cat in her arms.

Asher recognized her and felt cold guilt flush through his veins.

The last time he saw her, he executed her father right in front of her eyes. If she recognized him, she didn't show it.

"Hello there, Amy." Olander brushed past Asher and Malakai and kneeled down in front of the child.

Asher relaxed and let his hand drift away from his gun. The little girl might have a damn good reason to want him dead, but it was unlikely she was about to do the deed herself.

"Hi," Amy greeted cheerily. Her young, innocent eyes darted from Olander to Malakai, and finally to Asher. She studied him longer than she had the others, but he detected no recognition or hostility in her gaze. She appeared open, warm, and inviting in the way only a child can.

Asher didn't have a lot of experience with kids. He and Karen had never tried, and he and Larissa had never even talked about it. The gunslinger lifestyle didn't exactly seem conducive to having children.

Amy was a pretty girl, her hair tied in pigtails, wearing a loose-fit denim one-piece with pink suspenders. It made Asher wonder what his own daughter would be like, if he ever had one. And if he did, how would she feel if one day somebody gunned him down while she watched?

"That's a nice necklace you're wearing," Olander said. "Very pretty, just like you."

It was a typical silver chain necklace, not so tight that it would constrict around Amy's throat, but not loose enough to remove without undoing the clasp. The dangling jewel resembled a diamond but was blue in color, the shading so dark that it almost looked purple, like a bad bruise or the sky before a thunderstorm.

"Thank you. Mommy gave it to me." She moved her arms a little to better display the pet she was holding. "Daddy gave me the cat, but he's not here anymore." She said it matter-of-factly, but her eyes saddened.

Asher felt fresh guilt—or rather, old guilt resurrected—rip through him. He glanced over at Malakai, troubled. His friend gave him a sympathetic look.

Then Rene Perelli appeared, and Asher instantly forgot about past sins as he responded to present threats.

His hand found the butt of his gun again as Rene stopped behind her daughter, putting gentle hands on the girl's shoulders. She was dressed like she was going to a dinner party, all style and flash. She was the kind of ice-queen goddess that made men leer, but word on the street was that she had shown zero interest in romantic entanglements since her husband died.

She stared at Asher with unreadable eyes and murmured a greeting. "Hello, Gabriel."

Well, at least she wasn't going to come out with guns blazing. He relaxed his grip on the HK45. Doubtful they were going to shoot it out right here in the hallway with her daughter standing between them.

Truth was, the little girl's presence bothered him. He wanted to take out Rene Perelli for violating their truce and trying to kill him, but that would leave Amy an orphan. Dropping the hammer on Rene might be justified...but it would be an act of cruelty against the innocent child.

God, I hate this life sometimes.

Olander noticed him reaching for the pistol and held up her hand in a *wait-a-minute* motion. "Take it easy," she said. "This will all make sense in a moment."

"It damn well better," Asher growled.

"I mean you no harm," Rene said.

"You tried to kill me yesterday."

Rene tapped her daughter's shoulder. "Amy, take Purry and go get ready for school. I need to talk to this man."

"Who is he, Mommy?"

Rene glanced up at Asher. "Someone who used to work with your father."

Amy's eyes brightened. "You knew my dad, mister?"

Asher felt something in his throat constrict. He didn't trust himself to answer, so he just nodded. He had done a lot of hard things in his life, but facing this child of a man he had killed might just be the hardest of them all.

Malakai put a hand on his shoulder, firm and reassuring.

Rene watched him closely as Amy trotted off to her room, eyes slightly narrowed, and he wondered if she could sense his pain. He had come here to kill her—and still would, if it came down to that—but he still felt sorrow for what he had done to her, the husband he had stricken from her life.

In many ways, Asher knew he was responsible for the creation of Rene Perelli, mob queen. She had been nothing more than a gangster's housewife until he had forced her to rise from the ashes of the destruction he had brought upon their family. His bullet had brought down the king, so the queen had risen to power to take his place.

Olander interrupted his thoughts. "Let's cut right to the chase, shall we?" She looked at Asher and Malakai. "Ms. Perelli is working for us."

Malakai shook his head as if he couldn't believe what he had just heard. "You want to say that again?"

Asher's eyes narrowed to cold, glittering slits, but he didn't say anything.

"She's an informant," Olander replied. "She's working with the FBI to take down all the other East Coast families. The reasoning is that it's better to have one criminal organization operating with a government leash around its neck rather than multiple outlaw factions running around unchecked. We get a whole bunch of bad guys, and the Perelli organization avoids racketeering charges and long prison sentences. As long as they play by our rules, of course."

"Those rules...they include letting her attack me and Larissa?" Asher asked.

"I had nothing to do with that," Rene said. "I swear on my husband's grave."

"I ran the plates. They belonged to you."

"Somebody's trying to frame me."

"Think about it," Olander said. "Rene's enemies attack your house and make it look like she did it, knowing you would retaliate and take her out. They're setting you up to do the dirty work for them."

Asher considered the theory and grudgingly admitted that it was a possibility. "If that's the case," he said, "who do you think is behind it?"

"If I had to guess," Rene replied, "I'd say Sammy Quattro."

"Why him?" Malakai asked.

"I killed his son, so he wants me dead. Plus, he has ties to the Russians."

"The Crimson Cross?"

Rene nodded.

"Your last assignment," Olander said. "Uday Tunicov and his sex trafficking ring? That all went down because of information Rene provided." She looked at the crime queen. "Thanks again for that, by the way."

Rene responded with a slight nod. "No problem."

Malakai looked unimpressed. "Let's not start passing out the feel-good awards just yet. She's a criminal using the US government to knock her opponents off the game board and protect her interests. It's not like she's some kind of altruistic Good Samaritan."

"We're getting something out of it," Olander reminded him.

"Yeah, I heard you. It's the old *the enemy of my enemy is my friend* argument."

"Precisely. We're using one mob family to take down many. It's a sensible arrangement, and Ms. Perelli has held up her end of the bargain."

"Doesn't absolve all the shit she's done."

"I'm not asking for absolution," Rene said. "Also, let's not act like you and Gabriel are a couple of saints." She fixed her eyes on Asher. "In case we've all forgotten, he killed my husband."

"Trust me, I haven't forgotten anything," Asher said quietly.

Malakai looked at Olander. "I guess I can accept

that the Perellis weren't behind the hit on Asher, but that still leaves us with a problem."

"Right," Olander said. "Who *was* behind the hit, and how did they find him?"

"We've got a mole in Black Talon," Asher said.

"It does appear that way, I agree," Olander replied.

"Find the mole and we'll find out who organized the hit."

"We need to figure out the leak ASAP," Malakai said. "No more missions until we do. We're compromised from the inside, and you know what that means."

"Yeah," Asher growled. "We're totally fucked."

CHAPTER 13

DESPITE THE BITTER COLD, Sammy Quattro sat on his deck with its view of the Tappan Zee Bridge and listened to the winter wind rustle through the skeletal trees, thinking that they sounded like a dirge. He needed to pick up Nakano from the airport soon, a favor for their friends in Japan, but he had a little time to kill. He had come out here seeking peace, turning to nature for a brief respite from the pain of his son's death, but the bare branches rattling together like bones only served to remind him of all that he had so recently lost. The susurration of the icy breeze was sad and mocking, reminding him of what had been so brutally taken away.

Reminding him that a debt of vengeance was still owed against Rene Perelli.

He clutched his coat tighter around him and fired up a cigar. As the sweetly acrid smoke wafted into the air to be dispersed by the cold wind, his cell phone vibrated. Recognizing the number, he switched the cigar to his left hand and answered on the third ring.

"This is Quattro."

"Looks like Asher didn't take the bait," the person on the other end of the line said. "You fucked up."

Ordinarily, Quattro would have the speaker's tongue ripped out by the root for talking to him so disrespectfully. But the person on the other end of the line wasn't exactly ordinary.

"Yeah, our little trick didn't work," Quattro replied, tapping ash from his cigar.

"That's unfortunate."

"Shit happens."

The person on the other end of the line let out an irritated sigh. "Your plan might have worked, but Olander interfered."

"You should kill that bitch."

"Bumping off a senator isn't quite as easy as bumping off a mob queen."

"Bumping off a mob queen isn't turning out to be so easy, either. I should have taken a direct-action approach, gone at her head-on. I was trying to keep our hands clean."

"I'm not worried about keeping our hands clean," the caller said. "I'm worried about Perelli's deal with the FBI. It's designed to take out all the East Coast crime families, including you. If you go down and they discover my involvement with you, that puts me at serious risk."

"You're not much more than an information broker," Quattro said.

"I'm a lot more than that, and you know it."

"You worried? Want to call it quits and go our separate ways?"

"I think we're beyond that, don't you?"

Quattro shrugged, even though the caller couldn't see it. "Like I said, I'll come up with a new plan of attack."

"You damn well better. Make it happen."

"Of course I'm going to make it happen," Quattro snapped. "She killed my boy. I'm the one with real skin in this game, not you."

"The risk of going to prison means I've got skin in the game. This thing needs to get done sooner rather than later."

"It'll get done."

"When?"

"As soon as I can make it happen." Quattro didn't bother telling the caller that he badly, desperately, wanted Rene Perelli dead. Preferably, he could watch her die with his own eyes, but it didn't really matter, as long as he received confirmation that she was dead in a coffin.

But he also wanted her to suffer first. That was the part that wouldn't go over well with the person on the other end of the line. So Quattro kept silent about his plans.

Instead, he said, "I'll figure something out. That fucking bitch owes me a blood debt, and she's going to pay for what she did to Taide, that I promise you."

It wasn't just a promise to the caller. It was a promise to himself. He could fail a hundred times to execute Rene Perelli, and he would keep on trying until her head was no longer attached to her body.

"Very well," the caller said. "Try not to fail again."

Quattro almost snarled a "fuck you," but then decided provocation wouldn't accomplish anything. No point in testing the power dynamic between them. Sometimes silence was the strongest play.

The call ended without any goodbyes.

Quattro tapped ash from his cigar. He already knew what needed to be done. He had plenty of mad dogs at his disposal. Time to make them earn their keep.

CHAPTER 14

NAKANO NEVER CRAVED ATTENTION, but he could not help but attract it. Not just because of the black patch over his missing eye, but because he walked like a grim reaper sculpted from stone, as if chiseled by the hand of the devil himself. Lethality radiated off him in waves, and people sensed it, momentarily drawn to—and then repulsed by—his deadly, otherworldly demeanor.

In the vulgar vernacular of Americans, he was a scary motherfucker.

As he descended the escalator, wearing nothing but black, he made direct eye contact with anyone who dared to look at him. Without fail, they instantly turned away, instinctively realizing this was a man they wanted nothing to do with. Had he been given to self-satisfaction instead of stoicism, he might have smiled smugly.

He felt naked without any weapons but knew Samuele Quattro would have a cache waiting for him in the car. It had all been arranged. The only thing he carried with him at the moment was a small bag containing just enough clothes and accessories for a brief stay on this side of the ocean. Despite the reputations of Malakai and Asher, he really did not expect to be in this country very long. He would either kill them quickly, or they would kill him. It would not be a long, drawn-out process.

Quattro waited for him at the bottom of the escalator. Nakano walked over as the mob boss greeted, "Welcome to the Big Apple."

Nakano briefly wondered why the Syndicate tolerated the mob's presence in New York. They easily had the power and influence to drive the gangsters out of the city—out of the entire East Coast, for that matter—but for some reason, they let them remain in an unspoken treaty of sorts. But as quickly as the thought birthed in his mind, he aborted it. He was an assassin, nothing more. Leave the political maneuvering to those who grew fat in boardrooms rather than walk the killing fields.

"Can I take your bag?" Quattro asked.

Nakano shook his head. The movement was slow, methodical, almost robotic. "You have my weapons?" he asked.

"They're in the car," Quattro assured him. He jerked a thumb toward the exit. "This way."

Nakano followed him to the parking garage, where another man, wearing blue jeans and a black leather coat, leaned against the hood of a sleek, dark-blue BMW with tinted windows and a moon roof.

"I don't drive in the city," Quattro explained. "That's what I have Vinny here for. Hope that's okay with you."

"It does not matter," Nakano said.

"Plus, I needed someone to keep an eye on the weapons while I went inside to fetch you."

"I said it does not matter." The one-eyed assassin slid into the back seat while Quattro rode shotgun up front. Nakano remained silent until they had navigated their way out of airport congestion and then asked, "Where are they?"

Quattro half-turned in his seat to face the killer sitting behind him. "Which one you want first?"

"Shiomi is the primary traitor. Therefore, she is the primary target," Nakano intoned. "But I require locations for all of them."

"Right." Sammy faced forward again and fished out a cell phone. "I know where Asher lives, but I need to make a call to get Shiomi and Malakai's location."

"You do not possess the information I seek?"

"Not yet, but I'm about to get it. Hold your goddamned horses."

"You were informed I would be arriving and the purpose of my visit. I do not understand why you did not obtain the necessary information prior to my arrival."

"Busy making funeral arrangements for my son," Sammy said. "That all right with you?"

"I shall report your lack of competence to Fukuda-san."

"You do that. In the meantime, give me a second, and I'll get you the damned info."

Further away from the airport, the traffic thinned considerably. The driver hit the highway and headed north, swerving around slow-moving vehicles more erratically than Nakano would have preferred, but he endured in silence.

Quattro dialed a number. He didn't put it on speaker, but the voice on the other end came through loud enough for him to hear.

"Hello?"

"It's me," Quattro said.

"I know. That's the miracle of caller ID." The tone was cutting, impatient. "Didn't we just talk a couple of hours ago? I'm a little busy, you know."

"I need an address for Malakai and Shiomi, and I need it ASAP.

"How is that my problem?"

"Remember my guest from Japan? He's here, right now, in my car. He needs the address so he can do what he was sent here to do."

"You are becoming a serious pain in my ass, you know that? Maybe I should hire your Japanese friend to put you out of my misery."

"I don't need threats," Quattro snapped. "I need an address."

Nakano stared out the window and watched the passing landscape as the conversation continued. He felt frustrated that he was forced to deal with incompetent people, but kept the emotion firmly in check, locked down behind his usual stoic demeanor. He idly wondered whether or not he would kill Quattro when this was all over. Nakano prided himself on being a patient man, but he did not tolerate inefficiency well. Quattro's not having the target location identified upon his arrival felt like an affront, a deliberate disrespect. One that might merit a bullet or blade upon the conclusion of this mission.

"Getting involved with you was bad enough," the voice on the other end of the phone was saying to Quattro. "But getting into bed with the Syndicate? I must be a damn fool."

"Pretty sure you're being well compensated," Quattro said dryly.

Nakano stared at the back of the man's head. His eye roamed over the cranial surface, trying to decide exactly where he would place the bullet. If he chose to end Quattro's life, the old mobster would feel nothing, as if he had swatted a loathsome insect or washed some useless detritus down the drain.

"So when can I expect that info?" Quattro asked into the phone.

"When I'm goddamned good and ready. I have to call my contact."

Nakano's senses were exquisitely tuned to his surroundings. He imagined—or maybe it wasn't imagination—that he could hear Quattro's blood pumping through his veins, a bit faster than average, perhaps because of Nakano's nerve-racking presence. Maybe he should just stab him in the heart and be done with it.

"This is going to cost you extra," the voice on the phone said. "I hope you understand that."

"Yeah, yeah, I'll pay it."

"Damn straight you will."

Nakano found whoever was on the other end of the line irritating as well. Maybe he would kill them too.

"Sit tight," the voice ordered. "I'll get back to you."

"Make it fast," Quattro said, ending the call.

They sat in silence for the next several moments, a silence that quickly became awkward. But Nakano was perfectly comfortable with uncomfortable silences.

Vinny the driver kept his eyes on the road and his hands on the wheel, doing what he was paid to do, making a conscious effort to not look in the rearview mirror and meet Nakano's cold, single-eyed stare. Quattro drummed his fingers on the center console, a nervous tic that made Nakano want to chop his hand off at the wrist or maybe even the elbow.

Finally, after was seemed like forever but was probably less than five minutes, Quattro half-turned in his seat again, saying, "Look, fella, I gotta tell you..."

He presumably planned on telling Nakano that the whole situation was under control, and they should all just relax. But his voice trailed off into a hard swallow when the one-eyed assassin withdrew a sleek, shiny blade from under his jacket. Nakano did not bother telling him how and where he had acquired it. He just pressed it against the mobster's neck, directly above the Adam's apple.

"Whoa," Quattro said. "Take it easy."

"I do not like to be kept waiting, Mr. Quattro."

"The guy I'm talking to? He can get anything like that." Quattro snapped his fingers to show how quick it would be. "He'll call back in just a few minutes."

"If I do not have answers in the next three minutes, you may not have a head."

As if on cue, Quattro's phone rang. Nakano removed the blade from his throat so the mobster could answer.

"Yeah, hello?"

"Malakai and Shiomi currently live in Homosassa Springs, Florida," the voice said without preamble, and rattled off the address, which Quattro repeated for Nakano, even though the assassin could hear the other person just fine. Nakano committed it to memory. He did not need to write it down. "But only Shiomi is there right now. Malakai is currently in New York with Asher, meeting with Olander about the Perelli situation."

"Okay, thanks," Quattro said.

"Are we done here?"

Quattro glanced back at Nakano, who said nothing, but put away his blade to signify his satisfaction with the information.

Quattro sighed in visible relief and said, "Yeah, we're good." He ended the call and tossed the phone up on the dashboard.

"Take me back to the airport," Nakano commanded. "I need to get to Florida immediately."

"Malakai is here in New York," Quattro said. "Are you sure you don't want to handle him first since you're already here?"

"Shiomi is the primary target. She dies first. Turn the car around. I will not ask again."

"Whatever you say, pal."

Vinny got off at the next exit. He made a couple of left turns to pick up the entrance ramp for the southbound highway, and thirty minutes later, they were back at the terminal, swarmed by traffic, stopped dead in the drop-off lane. Nakano opened the door and swung his legs out.

"What about your weapons?" Quattro asked.

"I will acquire more when I reach Florida," Nakano replied. He offered no further explanation, just exited the car, closed the door, and vanished into the crowd like a magic trick. There one second, gone the next.

"Happy hunting," Quattro muttered, glad to be rid

of the creepy bastard. He almost felt sorry for this Shiomi bitch, whoever she was. Against Nakano, she was a lamb being hunted by a bloodthirsty wolf.

He didn't even want to imagine what the stone-cold killer with the black eyepatch would do to her.

CHAPTER 15

AMY WAS Rene Perelli's everything, a bright spot in a world of darkness, perhaps the only light she truly had left.

When she was with her daughter, Rene stopped thinking about her role as a criminal queen, the hard choices she had made, the life she had forged, and the lives she had taken. In those treasured moments, she was just a mom, a mother to the kindest, sweetest little girl who reminded her that she, too, had been innocent once, not all that long ago.

Sometimes she was tempted to keep Amy home from school, just to enjoy that feeling of innocence for an entire day. As head of the Perelli crime family, she had plenty of tasks to occupy her hours, but it was never enough to keep her from missing her little girl. They had grown even closer since her father's death at Asher's hands.

A black SUV pulled up to the front of the house, and Amy hopped in, giving her mom a quick wave goodbye. She looked forward to school. She was well-liked there, despite everyone knowing what her family did for a living, and Rene was grateful for that. The school did not believe that children needed to suffer for the sins of their parents. The teachers treated her just like any other kid and treated Rene just like any other parent who paid obscene amounts of money to send their children to the parochial school.

St. John's was a private Catholic school located one town over, and despite its rural location, it catered primarily to the rich and powerful. Grand archways guarded the entrance, and the grounds were immaculately landscaped, with towering statues of cherubic angels and stylized crucifixes, all topped with fluffy snow, like cotton candy wigs. In the warmer months, the flower beds bloomed with red and white roses. The school claimed the red represented the sacrificial blood of Christ, while the white symbolized the sin-cleansing salvation received from it.

Amy settled into the seat, adjusted the skirt of her school uniform, buckled her seat belt, and then waved at her mother again. "Bye, Mom!" she yelled just before the bodyguard closed the door.

Rene raised a hand in a farewell wave to her daughter as the bodyguard—Juliano, one of her best men, second only to Rabid—gave her a reassuring nod. It was the same every morning, a silent pledge that he would give his all to protect her. Two other guards joined him in the SUV, a three-man team with no other job than to keep Amy safe from any and all harm. If they failed, it was only because they were dead.

They would give their life for Amy. Of that, Rene had no doubt.

Seven hours later, Amy raced down the halls of St. John's, passing a stone statue of the saint for which the school was named, her necklace bouncing against her chest. Her rubber-soled shoes squeaked on the red-and-white checkerboard tiles. Children laughed and shouted and scurried around their cubbies, gathering their belongings at the end of the school day.

Amy grabbed her backpack and slid her arms through the straps. She held a finger painting she had done in class today because she did not want to shove it in her pack and have it get all crumpled. She couldn't wait to show her mom and put it on the refrigerator door with a magnet. She smiled at one of her teachers and headed outside.

Two of the bodyguards waited for her at the bottom of the wide stone steps. They wore dark coats and sunglasses, even though it wasn't that sunny out. Her driver, Juliano, held the door of the SUV open for her. She liked all three of the guys, but Juliano was her favorite. Sometimes he brought her a lollipop for the ride home.

Amy headed for the vehicle, walking between the two guards, but stopped when she heard a sound she didn't recognize.

Then the guard to her right fell down with his face blown open and blood splattering on the white cobblestone walkway. Some of the red droplets hit her face, and they felt hot and wet. She froze in place, a terrified shiver running through her small body.

The guard to her left roared, "Get down!"

Amy obeyed immediately. She dropped to the

ground, skinning her knees on the stones. She was so scared, she barely felt the pain.

Kids and parents stampeded everywhere, trying to get away from the gunfire. Amy crawled behind a large stone flowerpot and clamped her hands over her ears to drown out the noise. Her heart beat like panicked butterflies in her chest.

The guard who was still alive took a pistol out from beneath his jacket. Amy saw Juliano reach into the SUV and pull out some kind of short rifle. A submachine gun, she had heard it called. Gunfire continued to pour into the courtyard, slamming into the vehicles that were lined up and waiting to take the students home. Ragged holes appeared in the bodywork, and the windows exploded in sprays of glass.

Her peaceful school, the place she came to learn and play, had become a danger zone.

She still didn't know exactly where the gunfire was coming from, but two black SUVs, nearly identical to the one waiting for her, screeched to a halt in front of the courtyard. Juliano spun toward them as the doors swung open. Masked men with guns jumped out of both sides. Juliano managed to shoot one of them in the chest, but he was outnumbered and had to duck down behind his own SUV as return fire came his way.

The masked men were dressed in bulky gear that made them look like soldiers. One of them pointed right at Amy.

"Get that little bitch!"

The man had a heavy accent that Amy knew she had heard before, but she couldn't remember what it was called right now. Not when she was terrified for her life.

Her bodyguard opened fire on the assault team, trying to keep them at bay, but it was a losing battle. Juliano abruptly bolted away from the SUV and raced over to Amy. The other bodyguard's pistol ran dry. As he dropped down to one knee to swap the empty magazine for a fresh one, multiple bursts of enemy fire tore into him, chopping his body into a ragged mess of meat. He pitched over backward, dead within seconds.

Amy stared at him, horrified. She wanted to scream. There was so much blood.

"Get behind me!" Juliano shouted, pushing her down even closer to the ground and putting himself between her and the attackers.

For the first time, Amy realized Juliano's arm was bloody as well. It dripped like a leaky faucet from a hole in the sleeve of his jacket. Clearly, he had caught a bullet at some point during this mess.

He brought the submachine gun up to his shoulder and hit the trigger. One of the bad guys spun around like a top and fell to the ground so hard his nose smashed flat upon impact.

But more were coming. So many more...

Another long burst from Juliano. Another target went down, face and neck chewed up by bullets.

"We gotta make a run for it," Juliano said to her. "Do you understand?"

Amy could tell Juliano was trying to make his voice not sound scared, but it wasn't working, and that scared her even more.

"Do you understand?" he asked again.

"Yes."

"Good."

Her mother had made it very clear that in a

dangerous situation like this, Amy was supposed to do whatever the bodyguards said, no questions and no hesitation. They were there to protect her at all costs. Even if that cost meant dying for her.

More bullets chipped away at the stone flowerpot, and then came a lull in the gunfire.

"Now!"

Juliano lunged from cover and bolted for the far side of the courtyard, where a stand of birch trees would offer them more concealment. Amy stayed glued to his side, legs pumping to keep up with him. He fired his submachine gun as he ran, moving the muzzle back and forth in a wide pattern.

The bad guys' guns opened fire again. Almost immediately, Amy heard a meaty *thwack!* and watched in horror as Juliano fell down and slid along the ground like a baseball player trying to reach home plate. The holes in his neck—a small one where the bullet went in, a much bigger one where it came out—spurted bright-red blood.

Almost as red as the lollipop that fell out of his coat pocket. The lollipop that he would never give her again.

Sobbing and scared, she kept running as fast as she could, not looking back. She hated leaving Juliano like that, but she knew he was dead, just like her daddy. She was alone now, nobody left to protect her, and there were a whole lot of bad men coming after her.

She made it to the stone path that wound through the trees. Icicles dangled from the leafless branches like bony fingers reaching down to grab at her. She ignored the spookiness of her surroundings and kept on running. Not even thinking about a place to hide. Just trying to get as far away from the bad guys as possible.

She shrugged off her backpack, shedding the extra weight so she could run even faster.

It was all for nothing.

She had just reached the far edge of the trees when two masked men stepped in her path, grabbed her arms, and threw her down. She hit the ground with a loud, unladylike grunt.

She immediately began kicking and screaming like she was throwing the world's worst temper tantrum. Making fists and flailing her arms around, she managed to smack one of the men in the crotch. He groaned and tightened his grip. Much more pressure, and her wrist would snap like a dry twig.

"No! Let go of me!"

The two men hauled her toward a waiting SUV, leaving drag marks in the snow between the trees. The engine revved impatiently, ready to haul her away.

"Leave me alone!"

"Shut your mouth, kid, or I'll cut your tongue out," warned the one she had hit in the groin.

The other guy jerked her arm, and she felt something pop in her shoulder. She cried out in pain, but nobody cared. Plastic zip-ties went around her wrists and got snugged down so tight that they cut into her flesh, making her cry out again.

"I said to shut your mouth!" The guy backhanded her, his rough knuckles bruising her cheek. Her head whipped around from the force of the blow, and she tasted blood in her mouth where she had cut her lip against a tooth.

"Take it easy," said a voice inside the SUV. "We need her in one piece, at least for now."

"She punched me in the nuts."

"Yeah? Well, you *are* kidnapping her. I'd punch you in the balls too, if I were her. Now just toss her in the back, and let's get the hell out of here."

The men shoved her into the vehicle. Somebody slapped duct tape over her mouth. The door slammed closed, and one of the men said, "Package acquired. Let's roll."

Amy felt like her whole world was nothing but panic and pain. Tears streamed down her face. And then everything went black as the man next to her pulled a hood over her head. She heard the squeal of the tires as the vehicle rocketed forward. She silently cried out for her mother, knowing she couldn't hear her, but hoping, somehow, she could anyway.

Mommy! Help me!

She had never felt so alone.

CHAPTER 16

ASHER, Malakai, Senator Olander, and Rene Perelli sat in the same sunken living room where Asher had killed Peter Perelli not all that long ago. He could almost imagine the man's ghost hovering unseen over them, haunting and plaintive and hungry for some kind of revenge from beyond the grave. Asher idly wondered if the man's spirit was angry with his wife for forming a truce with his executioner instead of avenging his death.

Once Amy had shuffled off to school, Perelli had done as Olander instructed and brought Asher and Malakai up to speed on all the intel she could provide. They had been at it for hours, and it was now midafternoon. Asher had to admit that it was good information with valuable dirt on multiple high-level targets within the criminal underground. If they acted on everything Perelli was telling them, Black Talon would be busy for weeks, maybe months.

He had checked in with Larissa at the hotel, letting

her know he would be tied up for a while. She had confirmed both her safety and her boredom, but had promised him she would not leave the room. While it had become clear that Perelli had not attacked them at their house, *somebody* had, and until they figured out who had targeted them, neither of them was safe. The random hotel would have to be good enough for now.

So far, Rene had been cordial enough, but definitely frosty around the edges. Asher couldn't blame her and took no offense. It had to be extremely difficult to sit in the same room as the man who gunned down your husband. He certainly found it uncomfortable to sit in the same room as the wife he had widowed, to say nothing of the daughter he had orphaned. Even though fate had seemingly forced them to become arm's-length allies, neither of them wished to spend any more time than was necessary in each other's company.

The stark reality was, she would never trust him, and he would never trust her. Her strained cordiality wouldn't make him forget that. He didn't keep his hand on his gun at all times in her presence, but it was never far away, either.

Listening as Perelli rattled off more information about the various criminal factions plying their illicit trades in New York—not to mention neighboring territories like Vermont and even Canada—Asher wanted to be anywhere but here. Acid boiled in his stomach, and it wasn't entirely due to the coffee and pastries they had nibbled on earlier. Something deep inside him recoiled at being near her. Partially because of the guilt he felt over what he had done, partly because she had tried to kill him back in the day. Being around Rene Perelli made him feel like he was needlessly exposing himself to a lethal threat.

Perelli's phone buzzed. She glanced at the number and stood up. "Excuse me, I'll be right back." She stepped out of the sunken living room and walked down the hall, out of sight. Moments later, they heard her cry out, "No!"

Asher and Malakai both powered to their feet. The anguish in her voice was unmistakable. Something was wrong. They instinctively reached for their pistols, but Olander held up her hand, urging them not to overreact.

"Hold tight," she said. "Just wait until we know what's going on."

"No!" Rene cried out again. "No, no, no!"

"Whatever's going on," Malakai muttered, "it's safe to say that it isn't good."

Rene returned with the phone clutched in her bloodless, white-knuckled fingers. Her face looked just as pale. When her legs suddenly buckled, she had to lean against the wall for support.

"Shit," said Malakai. "What is it?"

"What's going on?" Asher asked.

Olander moved to Rene's side with an almost maternal look on her face. "Are you okay?"

Rene bit down on her lip so hard that it turned white. She looked as distressed as anyone Asher had ever seen, her face a long way from the cold, cutthroat mob queen she usually portrayed. Whatever the bad news was, it was personal, something more than a broken business deal or an operation gone bad.

Her glassy eyes barely contained the tears that

threatened to spill, like trembling drops of liquid silver hanging over an abyss from which they—and *she*—might never return. The fear, grief, and horror on her face made her look vulnerable. It was the same look Asher had seen right here in this very room on the night he assassinated her husband right in front of her—raw emotions and a broken heart combined with a white-hot fury.

"Rene, talk to me," Olander said. "Tell me what's wrong. What happened?"

The mob queen closed her eyes, and her voice cracked when she replied, "It's Amy. She's been taken. Somebody took my daughter."

Asher glanced at Malakai. He didn't have to struggle to know what his friend was feeling because they were *both* feeling it.

You don't mess with a child. In the game of gangsters, the kids were off limits, an unspoken but sacred rule. Only scumbags with no honor, no heart, no soul, targeted innocent children.

"The bastards," Rene said. "Those fucking piece of shit bastards."

"We'll get her back," Olander said. "And whoever took her will pay dearly."

"You got that right," Malakai rasped.

"Do we know who snatched her?" Asher asked.

"I'm sure the Perellis have plenty of enemies," Olander replied. "We'll need to narrow it down." She looked at Rene. "Did anyone see anything?"

"They didn't say. It all happened so fast."

"Does the school have security cameras?" Asher asked.

"If it's a ritzy private school," Malakai said, "then it'll have cameras out the ass."

"There are plenty of cameras," Rene confirmed.

Olander pulled out her phone. "I'll call Vesper, have her hack into the school's system, and send us the footage. She'll get it done quicker than going through the police."

Asher nodded. "Good idea."

Olander walked down the same hallway Rene had used a few minutes ago, speaking into her phone in low, urgent tones. She was back in less than a minute.

"I called the Church," she reported. "Vesper will send the footage to our phones ASAP."

"She say how long ASAP will be?" Malakai asked.

"No, but I imagine it will be *as soon as possible*." The senator gave him a look.

"Sorry," Malakai said, sounding anything but apologetic. "Patience isn't my strong point."

It felt like forever, but was actually only ten minutes before the security camera footage showed up on their phones. They huddled down and examined the footage together. There were multiple cameras aimed at the courtyard outside the school and the surrounding areas, all with varying angles, and many with overlapping fields that reduced blind spots.

They watched the brazen daylight kidnapping unfold in crystal clear resolution.

"They sent a lot of guys for one little girl," Malakai said.

"Maybe they didn't know how many guards they'd be dealing with," Asher said. "The whole thing looks like it was put together fast, impulsive, with minimal recon. So they sent more operators than necessary, banking on the overkill to make sure they pulled it off."

"Any ideas who they are?" Malakai asked.

"With them wearing masks, it's a waste of time to run the images through facial recognition software," said Olander. "But there must be something there."

"You mean you *hope* there's something there," Asher replied.

"Let's all zoom in and take a closer look."

Asher slowed down the footage and took his time, studying, looking for something—*anything*—that would identify the party responsible for abducting Amy Perelli.

And finally, he found it.

As they shoved Amy into the car, the mask on one of the men slid up and exposed a tattoo on the side of his neck.

"Damn." He paused the playback, enlarged the frame, and showed the image to Malakai. "You see that?"

"Shit."

"What is it?" Olander asked.

"A fucking cross," Malakai said.

"A *crimson* cross," Asher added.

Etched in ink on the kidnapper's neck, the symbol was unmistakable. The barbed wire cross, colored bloodred, revealed the Russian gang had snatched Amy outside her school.

Asher knew he and Malakai would hunt these fuckers down, but given the grisly reputation of the Crimson Cross, he didn't know if they would get to them in time to spare Amy. Hell, it was entirely possible she was already dead, but he kept the thought to himself. Rene might very well be thinking the exact same thing right now, but that didn't mean she wanted to hear someone say it out loud. They might not be friends, but that didn't mean he needed to inflict unnecessary pain on her. God knew he had done enough of that in the past.

"So it was the Russians," Rene said, glowering. "The goddamned Russians took my baby girl."

"Should have known those sons of bitches would be the ones willing to go after a child to get at the mother," Malakai growled.

Rene rubbed her temples as if trying to ward off the onset of a stress headache. "The Crimson Cross might have pulled off the actual abduction, but I don't think they're behind it."

"Who, then?" Olander asked.

"My guess? Sammy Quattro. He's been working with the Crimson Cross."

"But why would he target your daughter?" Asher asked.

Rene gave him a direct, level stare. "Because I killed his son."

"Did you have a good reason?"

"I had a reason, but I doubt it's good enough for you."

"Let's hear it, and I'll judge for myself."

"No," she said flatly. "You don't get to judge me. All you need to know is that he did this to get back at me. Right now, all that matters is finding Amy. And I know how to do it."

"How?" Olander asked.

"There's a tracking device inside Amy's necklace. That's why I make her wear it all the time."

"Hopefully, they don't take it away from her."

"No reason for them to. It just looks like an ordinary necklace."

"Is there a dedicated monitoring device?" Asher asked.

"It's an app," Rene said. "I can pull up her location on my phone, tablet, computer...pretty much any device. It's an upgraded version of those free GPS tracking apps anyone can download."

"God, I love technology," Malakai said.

"I'll have Vesper patch into the signal and track Amy from the Church," Olander said. "Once we know where she is, we might be able to get a satellite feed on her location that will give us better intel."

"Put a rush on it," Asher said. "We need to get her back before..."

He let his voice trail off as he saw the look of anguish on Rene's face. She knew all too well what could happen to her daughter, knew there was no guarantee that they would get her back alive, if they got her back at all. Again, it didn't need to be spoken out loud. Some things were better left unsaid, for everyone's sake.

Rene accessed the app on her phone. Within seconds, a map appeared with a pulsing blue dot showing Amy's location. It was moving south along Route 40, through the town of Greenwich. As they watched, it cut west toward Saratoga Springs.

"There she is," Rene said, unable to hide a tremor in her voice. "Where are they taking her?"

Olander was immediately on the phone, feeding information to Vesper.

"Hard to say," Asher replied. "My guess is they're heading for the Northway, and after that, who knows.

They don't know we're tracking them, so I expect them to hole up somewhere until the heat dies down, and then deliver Amy to Quattro."

"And once they hole up, we can hit 'em," Malakai said.

"Why not just hit them on the road?" Rene asked.

"Hard to do without them seeing us coming," Asher explained. "And if they see us coming, they could kill her on the spot, knowing the game is up. If we wait until they crawl into a hole somewhere, we can come up with a plan to take them by surprise. Gives us better odds for Amy's survival."

"So we just sit here and wait?"

"It's our best option."

"What if I say no? What if I want to send some of my security detail after them?"

"Can't stop you," Asher replied. "But if your guys get in our way when the time comes, it won't go well for them."

"Rabid, my head of security, knows what he's doing."

"Rabid?" Malakai snorted and shook his head. "Seriously?"

"It's a nickname, of course," Rene said. "And he's very good at his job."

"If he was good at his job, Amy wouldn't have been kidnapped," Asher retorted.

"Escorting her to school wasn't part of his duties."

"So where was he when this went down?"

"Here."

Asher pinned her with a hard, piercing stare. "So you kept your best man here at the house to protect you and sent the B team to protect your daughter? Am I reading that right?"

"Gabriel." Olander's voice held a warning. "Enough."

Rene met his gaze without flinching. "No, you're right," she said quietly. "I made a mistake, underestimated my enemies, and now my daughter is paying the price."

"Seems like children are always paying for the sins of their fathers," Malakai said. "Or, in this case, mothers. It's downright biblical."

"I recommend you have your men stand down," Olander said to Rene. "I'm sure they're good, but they're not in Asher and Malakai's league."

"We'll get Amy back," Asher said, silently adding, *Dead or alive. Hopefully the latter, but no promises.*

The next four hours passed with little movement or conversation. Rene sat and stared at the moving blue dot on her phone that symbolized her daughter's location, watching as it moved down I-87 and eventually picked up I-88 heading into the western part of the state. Then it merged onto I-81, heading north.

Asher and Malakai just sat and waited. There was little they could do at this point. Until they had a destination and target, they would remain idle, conserving their energy for the fight to come. They checked in with Larissa and Shiomi while Olander arranged to have weapons delivered to her jet at the airport, so they would be ready when the time came. Outside, the light devolved into shadows, and then the shadows lengthened as the darkness of evening descended on the world.

The dot stopped moving and stayed motionless.

Vesper called Olander's phone. The senator listened silently, then said, "Got it. You're positive on the location?" Pause. "Okay, thank you. We'll be in touch." She ended the call and faced her two operators. "We've got a location. An old farmstead in Steuben County. Vesper is uploading satellite images to your phones as we speak. You guys can evaluate and put an assault plan together once you're in the air."

"We taking your jet?" Asher asked.

Olander nodded. "Nearest airport to the target is Elmira-Corning Regional. I'll call the Church and arrange to have someone meet you on the ground with wheels once you land."

"Sounds like a plan."

"I'm going with you," Rene announced.

"The hell you are," Malakai snorted.

"I'm not asking for your permission. I'm telling you."

"No, hell no, and absolutely fucking not." Malakai shook his head. "Ain't gonna happen."

"You're not the only one with access to a plane," Rene reminded him. "Now that I know where Amy is, I can have Rabid and his team on their way just as fast as you. Either you let me tag along with you, or I send my own guys, and you can work around them."

"I'll work around them by putting bullets in their heads so they don't fuck shit up," Malakai growled. "Your daughter's life is on the line, lady. This ain't the time for amateur hour."

"I trust my men more than I trust you," Rene said.

"Then send them to fetch your kid, and we'll just sit back and watch."

"But," she added, "I do believe you and Asher are

more skilled at this sort of thing, so I would rather you do it. But I'm not just going to 'sit back and watch,' so you better start wrapping your head around the idea that I'm going with you."

"Listen," Olander said, "we're wasting time arguing when there are asses that need to be kicked and a little girl brought home."

"Then tell your snitch to sit down and let us do our job." Malakai was clearly getting frustrated.

Rene's eyes burned hotly. "What did you just call me?"

"I called a spade a spade," Malakai said. "You're ratting out your competition to maneuver yourself into a better position. You can sugarcoat it any way you want to help yourself sleep better at night, but in the end, you're just a snitch."

"Malakai," Asher interjected, "cut her a break."

"You want her tagging along with us?"

"No, but she's a mother trying to get her kid back, so I understand where she's coming from."

"She comes with us, she's just going to get herself killed."

"Didn't know you'd get all soft over the possible death of a mob queen."

"What about your little prayer?" Malakai asked. "Doesn't it say we don't kill women or children?"

"No, it says we don't kill *innocents*." Asher glanced over at Rene. "She's not innocent."

"I just want to be there when you find her," Rene said. "She's going to need her mother."

"She's not wrong," Olander said. "I hate to say it, but God only knows what they're doing to that poor child, and if she survives this, having her mother on-site will be beneficial."

Malakai looked at her as if she'd just sprouted another head. "Are you seriously suggesting that she join us on this strike?"

"Right now, I'm just suggesting it," Olander replied. "If you need me to change it from a suggestion to an order, I can do that."

"Unbelievable." Malakai jabbed a finger at her. "You're way off the reservation on this one, lady."

"And you're way out of line."

Asher stayed silent. Let Malakai and Olander fight it out. He could tell the writing was already on the wall. Rene Perelli had proven herself to be a valuable intelligence asset to the Black Talon program, and Olander would give her whatever she wanted, including a ride-along on the raid to recover her daughter. He understood Malakai's frustration—hell, he even felt it himself —but he figured his friend was just wasting his breath arguing.

"This is a fucking joke," Malakai said. "A goddamned clown show."

"It's my call, not yours," Olander replied.

"You may want to refresh your memories on our contracts," he shot back. "We have the right to refuse a mission."

"You can refuse to go," Olander acknowledged. "But you can't refuse to take her with you if you do go."

"We're playing semantics now?" Malakai shook his head. "For fuck's sake..."

Asher addressed Rene directly. "You understand getting Amy back is going to be dangerous, right?

They're not going to give her back just because we walk in there with a smile and a six-pack and ask nicely."

"I can hold my own," she huffed.

"I seriously doubt that," he said. "There could be twenty, thirty guys there for all we know, and every one of them will be looking to put a bullet in our asses. We're trained for this. You're not."

"I promise I won't get in your way."

"Lady, you're in our way just being there," said Malakai. He glowered at Olander. "This is a bad call, and you damn well know it."

"Perhaps. But like I said, it's my call to make."

Asher stared at Rene. "You don't belong. You must know that."

"My daughter is there. It's *exactly* where I belong."

"You do what we say, when we say it, no questions asked."

Malakai groaned, realizing this was going to happen whether he liked it or not.

"Of course."

"I mean it," Asher said, voice hard. "You pull any prima donna mob queen bullshit out there, I'll shoot out your knees and leave you there until we get back. We clear on that?"

"You will do no such thing." This from Olander.

Asher didn't even bother glancing at her. "Try me."

"You have a deal," Rene said.

"And we're not responsible for what happens to you. You need to make that clear to your men before we leave. I don't want you getting dead because you insisted on tagging along and then have your dogs declare some blood feud of vengeance."

"I'll tell them the decision—and the risk—is mine and mine alone."

"You know this is stupid, right?"

"You would understand better if you had children."

"Maybe," Asher conceded.

"This is a bad idea, Gabe," Malakai said. "You got a death wish or something?"

"Nobody lives forever."

"Great, just what we need before a mission—you going all fatalistic on me."

"I'm not fatalistic, I'm realistic." Asher slapped his friend on the shoulder. "Come on, let's go save a kid."

CHAPTER 17

ASHER AND MALAKAI geared up on the flight. Olander's pilots had been given explicit instructions to fly them to Elmira-Corning Regional Airport and not ask any questions, particularly about the copious firepower loaded onto the jet.

Whoever the Church had contacted to supply them with weapons had done a fine job. There was a little of everything: pistols, submachine guns, explosives, blades, grenades. It was an assassin's version of a candy store. Asher and Malakai strapped on some body armor and ballistic vests and perused the gun selection.

"They brought us some nice sidearms," Malakai said, surveying several SIGs, Glocks, and Berettas. "But I'm sticking with my FNX."

Asher nodded his agreement. His own HK45 pistol was already snugged into a drop-leg holster. Spare magazines were tucked into pouches on his ballistic vest. He had retrieved the SPAS-12 from his truck and brought it on board, but wasn't convinced it was the right tool for this job.

Malakai seemed to sense his thoughts. "Debating the Franchi?"

"Still mulling it over, but I'm not sure this is going to be a shotgun scenario."

Malakai preferred a Heckler & Koch UMP45 submachine gun for this kind of assault. Same ammo as his pistol and packed some serious knockdown power. A KA-BAR combat knife hung in a sheath on his left side, honed sharp enough to chop down a tree...or a human torso.

"My guess," he said, "is that you're gonna need something with a bit more range this time. Something a little more hush-hush too. Hard to put a suppressor on a shotgun."

"I think you're right."

Asher had two options to choose from. The first was an M4 Carbine equipped with all the fixings, including an EOTech sight, flashlight, rubberized grips, and suppressor. The second was an FN F2000, a Belgium-manufactured bullpup rifle with a sleek, wavy design that allowed the magazine to be inserted beneath the handle. Like the M4, it sported all the tactical bells and whistles.

"What are you going with?" Malakai asked.

"Thinking about going feral. Nothing but my bare hands and teeth."

"Ballsy. Stupid, since these Crimson Cross dipshits will have an arsenal. But definitely ballsy."

Asher patted the M4. "I'll bring the carbine for backup. You know, just in case the bare hands and teeth thing doesn't work out."

"Probably a wise move."

They double-checked all their equipment, observed keenly by the other person on the plane with them.

"Anyone care to help me gear up?" Rene Perelli asked.

"If you need help, you shouldn't be here," Asher replied.

"We've been over this, and it's not up for debate."

"Look around." Asher gestured around the jet's interior. "Olander isn't here anymore to run interference. If I decide to leave your ass on the tarmac when we land, there's nothing you can do about it."

"I can take care of myself, you know."

"Really? Because you just asked for help picking out weapons."

Rene gave him an eye roll that would have made a teenage girl proud, grabbed the FN F2000, and slapped a magazine into the well. With her finger properly staged outside the trigger guard, she asked, "Since you're not using this one, can I have it?"

"Just try not to shoot me in the back with it."

"You really don't think I'm ready for this, do you?"

"Is that a question?"

"Not really. Just stating the obvious."

"I *know* you're not ready," Asher replied.

"I can handle myself, and that's the truth."

Malakai cut into the conversation. "Like you know anything about truth."

"What's that supposed to mean?"

"It means you're a criminal."

"What?"

"You heard me," Malakai said. "Really, you're not much different from the guys we're on our way to kill. Sure, you come in a prettier package, but when you get right down to it, you're just a gangster who runs drugs and guns, launders money, orders people killed. You're not the solution. You're part of the damn problem."

"You think you're better than me?" Rene scoffed. "Yes, I've ordered people killed. But you two? You two actually *do* the killing. Your hands are covered in blood, and let's not pretend otherwise, gentlemen."

"We only kill people who have it coming," Asher said.

"We all have it coming, don't we?" Rene shook her head. "Whatever helps you sleep at night."

"Jack Daniels and a good woman, that's how I sleep at night."

"A good woman you still have because of the truce I made with you." Rene's eyes flashed dangerously, reminding him that she was not someone to be trifled with. You did not rule a mob family as a woman without possessing serious grit, steel, and ruthlessness. "I could have taken her from you by now, just like you took my husband from me."

"A truce you made with a gun to your head," Asher replied. "Ain't no angels riding this plane, so let's not pretend you're some kind of saint who spared Larissa out of the goodness of your heart."

"Maybe not, but I still spared her. And now I'm putting my daughter's life in your hands, even after what you did to my husband." She pinned him with her gaze. "You took one life from me. Now you can give one back."

Asher felt the words cut deep, like a surgical blade slicing down to where flesh and bone meet a man's essence. The bloody image of Peter Perelli crucified against the wall as the bullet blew through his head rose unbidden in his mind. He could still hear the heart-broken sobs of a little girl—a little girl he was now trying to save—stinging his ears. Peter might have deserved to die for his sins, but not in front of his family. The kill still haunted Asher. He had no excuse for how he had handled it.

"This the part where you tell me you're not the same man anymore?" Rene asked.

"That what you want to hear?"

"I don't need to hear it. I can see it."

"Don't act like you know me."

"I know enough."

"Think what you want," Asher said. "Gear up and be ready to move as soon as we're wheels down."

"What's the catch?"

"No catch. I'm just done arguing with you. If you want to get your ass shot off, be my guest."

"I don't care about me. I only care about Amy."

"Guess that's one thing we can agree on," he said. "She's the only one that matters right now."

"Gabriel." Rene's voice became soft, fragile, plead-ing. All traces of the gangster queen vanished, and in its wake, there was nothing left but a frightened, desperate mother. "We have to get her back."

"That's the plan," Asher replied. "That's the plan."

CHAPTER 18

"YOU GAVE permission for *who* to tag along on this mission?"

Congressman Brody Anderson delivered the question with such ferocity that Senator Olander pulled the phone away from her ear as if the volume of the politician's furious voice might rupture her eardrums. It made her angry. Who the hell did this rookie asshat think he was talking to?

"You heard me," she snapped. "Rene Perelli is on the plane with Asher and Malakai as we speak."

"Rene Perelli, the head of the Perelli crime family."

"Yes."

"You gave permission for not just a civilian, but a *criminal* civilian, to accompany our operatives on a classified operation? Have you lost your damn mind?"

"It's her daughter. Plus, she threatened to stop cooperating with us if we didn't allow her to go. Since you somehow managed to weasel your way into this program, you know how valuable her intel has been."

"I don't like it," Anderson growled. "Not one little bit."

"I really don't care if you like it or not," Olander retorted. "It was my decision to make. I run this program, not you. Far as I'm concerned, you're just a political butt-kisser who doesn't belong anywhere near a program like this. How'd you hear about this mission, anyway? We put it together damn fast, on the fly, and yet somehow, you're already in the loop."

"Who do you think?" Anderson said. "Vice President Steinbeck told me."

"Yeah, well, I wish he hadn't done that, but it doesn't change anything. Bottom line is, I don't need to explain myself to you, Mr. Anderson. Last time I checked, I don't answer to you. So do us both a favor and stay in your lane, and tell him I said he should stay in his too."

"Him?" Anderson echoed in disbelief. "You mean the vice president?"

"Yes, the VP," she replied. "When the president wants to call and tell me to stand down, maybe then I'll listen. But I don't answer to the VP. If you paid attention to how this program operates, you'd know that. But you're too busy trying to prove you've got a bigger dick than me."

"You are fucking with the wrong guy." Anderson's voice was quiet and cool, but you could still tell he was seething. "I have the ear of Vice President Steinbeck, and he has the ear of the president, which means I have the ear of the president."

"I think you're seriously overestimating how much of that ear Steinbeck has," Olander said. "Which means you're seriously overestimating *your* power. Honestly, Brody, you're a kid playing with a toy truck in a sand-box, thinking you've got the biggest machine, completely oblivious to the fact that everyone else has bulldozers and is about to flatten you like a roadkill pancake."

"If you think I can't do serious damage to your precious Black Talon program, you're dead wrong, Senator."

Olander sighed, making sure her exasperation trans-mitted through the phone. "This is where I tell you to take your best shot, Brody. Are we done here, or should I just hang up like I should have done the second I heard your voice?"

"Oh, we're done for now," Anderson said. "But the game is just beginning."

"Let me just make one thing clear. Anything happens to my guys, I'm going to assume you were behind it, and I'll be coming for you. And by the time I'm done, you'll be begging the devil to take you to hell, just to get away from me."

She didn't wait for a reply. Just ended the call.

Stupid bastard.

Only a fool crossed swords with someone who had two elite assassins at her disposal. If Congressman Anderson turned up the heat or stepped dangerously out of line, she wondered if she could convince Asher or Malakai to do what needed to be done. They both followed a strict code—The Assassin's Prayer, named for his first wife, who had written it on a napkin for him —and it was a code Olander generally respected, accepted, honored, and followed herself.

But she wasn't naïve. She also knew that sometimes, on rare occasions, even the most sacred codes needed to be broken. On rare occasions, even the innocent must be sacrificed for the greater good.

And if he didn't tread very carefully, Brody Anderson was going to make himself a rare occasion.

CHAPTER 19

OLANDER'S private jet made good time. One of the pilots announced they would be on the ground at Elmira-Corning Regional Airport shortly, local time 9:15 p.m.

Asher, Malakai, and Rene conducted another round of equipment checks, getting ready for the extraction. Asher felt his stomach drop as the jet dipped lower to line up for the landing. Thank God he didn't suffer from motion sickness. He had known operatives who needed Dramamine in order to fly without vomiting all over the place, but the medicine's after-effects sometimes left them slightly sluggish. In the killing game, microseconds mattered. Personally, Asher would have puked in a paper bag the whole trip before popping any pills.

He snugged his .45 into its holster and saw Malakai doing the same. His friend's UMP45 was strapped across his chest with a tactical sling. Asher slung his M4 Carbine over his shoulder for the time being. Rene had armed herself with the FN F2000, a Beretta 9mm pistol, and an Ontario fixed blade knife similar to Malakai's KA-BAR. They would all be ready to roll when the wheels touched down.

He glanced at Rene. He had stopped trying to convince her to stay behind, but that didn't mean he believed she was ready for what lay ahead. She looked broken, slumped in her seat, staring out the window at the night sky. The fires of rage still burned on her face and in the steely glint of her eyes, but those flames could not conceal her distress. She was doing her best to hide her emotions, but the hurt, the pain, and the fear were visible to anyone who cared to look for them.

No surprise there, Asher thought. Rene was a mother, and her child had been taken, quite possibly the single worst nightmare for a parent. Despite her best efforts, she was probably thinking terrible thoughts, imagining her little girl crying, tied up, alone, maybe even tortured, begging, screaming for someone to help her. Those were the kind of mental images that would drive a mother insane.

Reflected in the window, Asher saw Rene's lips moving and could just barely make out the whispered words.

"Don't worry, baby. Mommy's coming."

The words were spoken much like a prayer and contained so much suffering. Asher might not have kids, but he knew what it was like to lose loved ones. His first wife had been taken from him by the murderous hands of a madman, and he had nearly lost Larissa when she took a bullet to the head during their confrontation with Colonel Macklin.

Rene had already lost her husband, thanks to Asher, right in front of her eyes, which meant Amy was all she had left. He felt confident they could get her back, as long as she was still alive. He and Malakai knew how to strike hard, strike fast, and get results.

But while he was confident, he refrained from *over*confidence. This game was dangerous, the Crimson Cross were ruthless butchers, and any mission could go sideways in a single heartbeat and without warning. The gods of war were fickle bastards at the best of times.

He wanted to tell Rene that her child would be safe and back in her arms soon. But he didn't, because he knew those words could very well turn out to be lies. There was no guarantee that any of them were getting out of this alive. So he kept quiet and let her whisper her prayerful words at her reflection in the glass.

"Don't worry, baby. Mommy's coming."

Asher vowed right then and there to put it all on the line. Not for Rene, or Olander, or himself, but for a little girl he had robbed of a father. Call it atonement, call it redemption, call it whatever the hell you wanted, but he was going to do his damnedest to get her back.

He was not much of a praying man, but if any half-formed prayers ghosted through his mind at that moment, they were for her.

Malakai seemed to pick up on his pensiveness and asked, "Your head in the game, buddy? You ready for this?"

Asher turned away from Rene and faced his friend. "That little girl needs to come home."

"That's the plan."

"And everyone who took her dies."

"That's also the plan."

The descent into Elmira-Corning went smoothly.

The jet's wheels touched down with the screech of rubber hitting asphalt, and moments later, they were taxiing onto the tarmac.

Rene seemed to shake herself out of her reverie. "We're here."

"Yeah," Asher said. "Game time."

The captain brought the jet to a halt, and then the copilot quickly exited the cockpit to lower the passenger stairs. The cold air of the night rushed in at them, the stiff breeze carrying an icy bite. Western New York at this time of year wasn't quite as cold as the Adirondacks that Asher called home, but it was a long way from tropical.

"Hope Olander managed to arrange a ride for us," Malakai said.

"She's not my favorite person," Asher replied. "But she always delivers when it comes to support."

"Let's do this." Malakai stepped out of the jet and walked down the stairs.

Asher followed him and spotted the two black SUVs parked nearby, engines idling, smoke puffing from hot exhaust pipes into the frigid air. The headlights flashed on, washing them in the white glare. It was impossible to see the driver or any of the occupants, but Asher doubted he would know them anyway. They would be local talent recruited by Olander, paid to chauffeur them to the target and ask no questions. Asher hoped they were professional enough to do just that and nothing more. He also wished they would turn their damn high beams off. The glare blinded him.

Carrying their gear, they started walking toward the vehicles, Asher and Malakai side by side, Rene a few steps behind. Still, nobody exited the SUVs. Asher shook his head. They were dealing with amateurs. Even a semi-professional pickup team would have had at least two men outside the vehicles performing area security, scanning for threats.

Malakai suddenly stopped. Clearly, his hackles were up. "Something's wrong."

"Yeah," Asher muttered. "They sent idiots to drive us."

"I don't think they're idiots, I think..." Malakai let his voice trail off as his hand slid closer to his holstered pistol.

Asher felt something deep in his guts clench tight.

"What is it?" Rene asked. "What's wrong?"

"You in the car!" Malakai yelled. "Turn off the lights and step out where we can see you."

Nothing happened.

Asher felt his pulse quicken. His heart rate kicked up a notch. His thoughts were all bad. He was sorely tempted to use the M4 to dump a whole magazine through the windshield of the closest SUV. Wipe out the threat before it even became one. Problem was, he couldn't be sure it *was* a threat. He couldn't kill a bunch of people based on gut instinct alone.

A few more seconds ticked by, and then he got his confirmation.

The doors of both SUVs opened at the same time, and men armed with submachine guns boiled out onto the tarmac.

Not an escort.

A goddamned ambush.

"Go, go, go!" Malakai pushed Rene back toward the jet.

Asher whipped the M4 into play, sending a burst

sizzling into a gunner's chest and neck. He swung the carbine left to right, dancing the salvo across the windshield. The dead driver thrashed behind the wheel as bullets perforated his face, blood splattering everywhere.

Return fire came Asher's way. It was hasty and missed the mark, but not by much. He couldn't just stand out here in the open like some old west gunslinger. He needed to fall back and find cover. The jet was the closest option. There was a small utility shed nearby with a silver Toyota Camry parked next to it, but they would have to cross nearly one hundred meters of open tarmac to reach it. With a kill team unleashing full-auto hell on their asses, that move would be a sucker play.

The jet would have to suffice for now, and they would just have to hope Lady Luck wasn't being a rotten bitch tonight.

Malakai shoved Rene behind the jet's stairway and crouched down next to her. It wasn't ideal cover, but it was better than nothing. Asher dropped down behind the front wheel, which offered even less cover, and tried to count how many hostiles they were facing. Best he could tell, it was a ten-man hit team.

Two down, eight to go...

"Shit, we're fucking cornered," said Malakai.

"I can see that," Asher replied.

"Somebody fucked us over." A fresh barrage of enemy bullets bounced off the stairway with a rapid series of *thunk-thunk-thunk* noises.

"Tell me something I don't know."

"How the hell did they know to hit us here? We've got a fucking leak, man. Somebody is fucking us, hard."

"Yeah," Asher rasped tersely. There was nothing else to say. They were in the thick of a firefight with the odds stacked against them. Bitching about the betrayal that had put them in this situation could wait until later. Right now, all they could do was try to survive.

Anger burning through him, Asher leaned out and got his sights on a target. His finger moved quickly on the M4's trigger, once, twice, double-tapping the enemy gunner crouched by the front bumper of the nearest SUV. The man went down with a pair of holes drilled in his heart. Blood misted in front of the headlights, giving the glare a red tint.

Down to seven.

With better cover, Malakai took the time to zero in on the second, further away, SUV. He hit his target with savage accuracy, putting a couple of .45 slugs from the UMP into the man's center mass. The guy threw up his arms, weapon sailing off into the night, and toppled backward. If he wasn't dead before he hit the ground, it wasn't long after.

Four down, six left.

The odds were getting better, but Asher knew they couldn't stay here. The position was unsustainable unless they wanted to be massacred. If these guys had been professionals instead of the Crimson Cross mutts he assumed they were, they would be dead already. He briefly considered trying to reboard the jet and take off, but he knew the plane's thin aluminum shell did not provide sufficient cover to protect them. The bullets would punch right through, and they would be shredded by enemy gunfire before the jet could even start to taxi down the runway.

They were pinned down like sitting ducks.

They needed to get the fuck out of here.

He got Malakai's attention and pointed at the Toyota Camry parked by the shed. "I'm going for the car!"

"Are you shitting me?"

"You got a better idea?"

Rene held the Beretta pistol in her hand but had not yet fired a shot. She didn't look shaken up, just concerned. Understandable, given their position.

Malakai glanced at the Camry, shook his head, and then said, "Fuck it. I'll cover you. Go!"

The enemy gunners were advancing, leapfrogging forward, firing as they came. Bullets sparked off the jet's wheel assembly. Malakai leaned out from behind the stairs and triggered a chopping burst across a man's lower legs. Crippled by shattered shinbones, the target fell forward and caught the follow-up bullets in the top of his head. His obliterated skull smacked the ground with a soggy splat.

Five tangos terminated, five more to go.

Teeth gritted, Asher lunged from behind the wheel assembly and ran as fast as he could toward the car. His feet pounded the tarmac as if the hounds of hell were snarling at his heels.

Malakai provided covering fire, and Rene joined the fray, the Beretta bucking in her fist. He didn't notice her hit anything, but that didn't matter right now. What *did* matter was keeping the Crimson Cross shitheads from drawing a bead on Asher. They succeeded in driving three of the bastards back toward the cover and concealment of the SUVs. But two stood their ground and triggered salvos in Asher's direction.

Asher was smart enough not to run in a straight

line. He zigged and zagged his way to the Camry as bullets buzzed around him. He kept moving, ducking, weaving, knowing the second he stopped, he was most likely a dead man. The Kevlar vest might protect his torso, but wouldn't do jack-shit if he caught a slug upside the head.

His luck held, and he reached the sedan. He paused long enough to spin around and fire a quick burst from the M4 at the pair of gunners hurling rounds his way. He hit one of them in the face, splitting it open like a hatchet. The other one flinched as his buddy's brains splattered on him like clumps of hot, wet dog food.

Asher glanced at the jet and saw that Malakai and Rene were still holding their own behind the stairway.

He trusted his partner to take care of himself and focused on the task at hand. He almost shot out the window to gain access to the car, but decided to try the handle first. Luck continued to roll his way, and the door opened. He quickly slid behind the wheel, reached for the ignition, and snarled a curse.

No fucking key.

Contrary to how it was depicted in the movies, hot-wiring a car wasn't easy. He could do it, given enough time, but time was something he didn't have right now. Not with bullets hunting his ass.

He flipped down the visor, hoping to get lucky again.

Nothing.

Shit!

Of course it couldn't be that easy.

He leaned over to check the glove box. Just in time too. A bullet starred a hole in the rear window and punched through the headrest. He flinched—*I really need to get this car fucking moving!*—and opened the compartment. Nothing but a dog-eared user's manual and a crumpled pile of fast-food napkins. He swept them both aside, hoping the key might be hidden underneath them, but no luck.

He sat back up, hoping he didn't catch a bullet in the back of the head, mind racing. Only one more place to check.

He reached down and felt around under the seat. His fingers fell on something furry. He dragged it out and saw that it was a rabbit's foot keychain with a single key dangling from the brass ring.

Gotcha.

He plunged the key into the ignition, and the Camry came right to life, engine thrumming as he revved the gas pedal. He slammed the car into reverse, whipped it around, and gunned it across the pavement. He heard slugs pounding the bodywork as he raced toward the jet. Malakai and Rene leaned out from behind the stairway to open fire on the ambushers. They didn't score any hits, but the salvos were enough to keep the remaining Crimson Cross SOBs hunkered down behind their SUVs.

Over half the kill team was eliminated, but that still left at least four guns to hammer away at them. The bastards popped up from behind the SUVs like gun-wielding gophers to trigger short bursts and then ducked back down behind cover.

Asher wanted to roll down the window, stick out his pistol, and start sending lead their way. But he kept his hands on the wheel. Right now, Malakai and Rene were responsible for the gunning. His job was to drive the escape vehicle.

He stomped the brake and drifted the Camry like he was in some kind of illegal street race, sliding to a stop near the jet's stairway. Bullets hammered the car, and more holes popped in the back window.

"Get in!" he yelled to Malakai and Rene. He whipped around in his seat and used his .45 to fire out the busted rear window, trying to provide enough cover fire for the two of them to make it to the car. He saw one of the thugs go down with a hole in his forehead.

But that still left three. One of them opened the hatch of the furthest SUV.

Bullets strafed the stairs, keeping Malakai and Rene pinned down, unable to make a break for the car.

Malakai's pistol ran dry. He ejected the spent magazine and plucked a fresh one from his vest. As he slammed it up the well, he saw the man at the back of the SUV reappear, stepping around the side of the vehicle.

"Shit!" Asher snarled.

The son of a bitch raised a Milkor MGL 40mm grenade launcher to his shoulder and aimed at the Camry.

Asher bailed out of the car as the launcher belched a grenade. He threw himself to the ground and rolled as the mini-bomb punched through the shattered back window and plowed into the driver's seat. The Camry exploded in a cascade of flames and shrapnel. Fiery wreckage rained down as Asher kept rolling, desperate to get out of the blast radius. Somehow, he managed to keep hold of his pistol. Heat scorched the back of his neck.

He heard the sharp screech of tires as he used his momentum to power up into a half-kneeling, half-crouching position. Another SUV barreled out onto the tarmac. Men leaned out the windows, guns bristling in their hands. Looked like the Crimson Cross assholes had called for backup. The bastards were like cockroaches. You killed one, and five more appeared.

Asher snarled a curse. They were royally screwed. They'd been lucky up until now, but every warrior knows luck runs out and fate turns on a fucking dime. He had always known he would meet his end somewhere, but he had not expected it to be on the tarmac of a small-town airport.

Over the crackle of flames, from inside the jet, he heard the captain shout, "Get in here, and I'll try to get us airborne!"

The grenade launcher guy swung the weapon toward the plane.

"No!" Asher yelled, triggering three fast shots from his HK45.

The rounds ripped into the man's ribcage and ravaged his vitals...but not before he fired the launcher.

The grenade sailed through the open doorway and detonated inside the jet. The cockpit exploded in a fury of flames and twisted steel, killing the pilots instantly.

The backup SUV skidded to a halt and a half dozen Crimson Cross goons poured out of it. One of them grabbed the fallen grenade launcher out of the dead man's hands.

Asher was running toward Malakai and Rene, who were both still crouched under the stairway, the only cover and concealment available. He fired on the run and without really aiming, blowing a couple of holes in the newly arrived SUV's radiator and popping one of the headlights, but none of the bullets found any flesh.

"Looks like we lost our ride," Malakai said grimly.

"We're about to lose everything," Asher replied, jerking his chin toward the new guy raising the Milkor MGL to his shoulder. "Gotta move. Now."

They bolted under the jet and ran back toward the runway. The woods on the far side offered their only hope of escape. The Russian grenadier drilled an explosive right into the jet's fuel tank. The aircraft erupted into a huge, boiling ball of flame.

They used the explosion for cover, running as fast as they could for the trees. Not being in prime physical condition like the two assassins, Rene naturally fell behind.

Malakai looked over his shoulder and saw gunners fanning out on both sides of the burning jet. Their submachine guns blazed despite the distance, and one of them got lucky. Rene caught a bullet in the shoulder, twisting her around. The Beretta flew from her grip as she cried out in pain and fell to her knees.

"Rene!" Malakai yelled.

In the lead, Asher heard the shout, halted, and rushed back.

"She caught one in the shoulder," Malakai said. "Looks like a straight through, in and out, no bone damage."

"I've got her." Asher looped Rene's good arm over his shoulders. "We've gotta keep moving, or we're all gonna have some serious bone damage...in our skulls."

"I'm fine," Rene said, but the blood streaming from the wound and her pain-twisted face told a different story. "I can make it."

More bullets sizzled their way. Asher felt them scorching the air all around. Rene suddenly cried out and stumbled against him as a slug pierced her leg. She slumped out of his grasp and sprawled on the ground. He kneeled beside her as Malakai used the UMP45 to send return fire back at the Crimson Cross bastards.

The bullet had torn open the meat of her left thigh, carving a deep, bloody trench through the flesh and tissue. Possibly had even clipped the bone, but it was too much of a mangled mess to tell. Either way, she wasn't walking anywhere.

Damn it all to hell, Asher thought. *We're going to die on this fucking runway.*

Then something slammed into his head and the world went black as death.

CHAPTER 20

ASHER OPENED his eyes to find himself staring up at tree branches and beyond them, stars scattered like diamonds across a cold, black, velvet sky. But the stars shimmered and blurred and pulsed to a raging, painful rhythm in his skull. It felt like the worst hangover in history, multiplied by a factor of ten.

He slowly sat up, a groan dragging out from between his lips. Fighting back a surge of nausea, he saw Malakai leaning against a nearby oak tree, watching him.

"You look like shit," his friend announced.

"You always know just what to say to make a guy feel better." Asher touched a hand to his throbbing head. His fingers came away sticky with blood. "What happened?"

"Bullet creased your noggin. Knocked you out."

Asher glanced around. They were just inside the woods. Out on the tarmac, the jet still burned, so he couldn't have been out long. "Where's Rene?"

"They took her."

"She's dead?"

"No, I mean they took her. Like, captured her."

"That doesn't make..." Asher sighed. "Maybe you should just tell me what happened."

"She was down for the count with those bullets in her leg and shoulder, barely conscious, couldn't walk. And you were out cold." Malakai's face was grim. "I had to make a choice, you or her, so I left her there and dragged you to the woods. Figured if I got a chance, I would go back and get her."

"Not fucking likely with those bastards closing in."

"Exactly. By the time I got you to the woods, they were already dragging her away."

"They didn't keep coming for you and me?"

Malakai shook his head. "Once they got their hands on her, it was like they didn't care about us anymore."

"So we weren't the target," Asher said. "She was."

"Looks that way from where I'm standing."

"What the hell is going on?"

"Your guess is as good as mine."

"You call this clusterfuck in yet?"

Malakai nodded. "Talked to Olander."

"She have any insight?"

"I told her we got ambushed, and she said, 'That arrogant little cocksucker.' When I asked her who she was talking about, she said not to worry about it, that she would deal with it."

Emergency vehicles swarmed the burning jet and Camry, lights strobing the night with flashing reds and blues to accentuate the orange haze from the flames. They watched from the woods as local cops and state troopers examined the dead bodies strewn across the tarmac. Shouldn't take them too long to figure out they were dealing with Crimson Cross corpses, but they would definitely wonder how a US senator's private jet was involved.

Asher leaned against a tree and willed the jack hammering inside his skull to subside. He knew he was lucky to be alive, but he still felt a brokenness that surprised him. They had been compromised once again, and now Rene was gone, suffering who knew what at the hands of those cutthroats. Why he felt responsible for her, he wasn't sure, but losing her made him feel like he had lost part of his team.

You're being stupid, he told himself. *She knew the risks, she took 'em, and she paid the price. Don't put this blame on your shoulders and carry it around like some kind of fucking cross.*

"We just got our asses kicked," Malakai said.

"We're still alive." *Well, except for Rene, maybe.*

"If it wasn't for that little girl, I'd be telling Olander to fuck off with any missions until she figures out why we keep getting compromised."

"Yeah, I know," Asher said. "But not really an option at this point."

"Maybe it's time to call it quits with Talon and take our chances."

"You might be right. But first things first, we have to get Rene and her kid back."

"What's the plan?" asked Malakai.

"Save their asses and kill everyone who had a hand in taking them."

"From your lips to God's ears."

"Amen," Asher said.

CHAPTER 21

SHIOMI RARELY STOPPED THINKING about Malakai when he was away on a mission.

It wasn't that she hated being alone. She wasn't some weepy, clingy girlfriend who didn't know how to exist without her man beside her at all times. She had been through a lot in her life—had been through *hell*—and developed the strength to stand just fine on her own, thank you very much.

No, she wasn't with Malakai because she *needed* him. She was with him because she *wanted* to be. Their love was mutual, not parasitic. They both carried deep scars on their souls that they rarely talked about, and they found comfort in each other. She'd had hundreds, maybe thousands, of "lovers" in her previous life as a Syndicate prostitute, but until Malakai entered her orbit, she had not known what it felt like to truly love and be loved. He had changed everything for her.

She stayed occupied by exercising in their home gym, followed by a shopping trip to the mall and an early matinee movie. She told herself that she was trying to keep her mind off Malakai and where he might be, what he might be doing, but that was a lie. Truth was, she was trying to distract herself so she wouldn't have to think about what she had done.

She had killed Nick Caesar. Yes, he was—or rather, had been—a disgusting, perverted, abusive bastard who deserved what he got. But that didn't change the fact that she had blood on her hands just the same.

She wondered if anyone had found his body yet. She considered Googling his name to see if he showed up on any police reports in Miami, but decided not to waste her time. Plus, if anyone ever suspected her of the slaying, it wouldn't look good to have recently conducted an online search for him.

She'd delivered justice, or revenge, or punishment, or whatever you wanted to call it. That was all that mattered. The creep got what he deserved, and that was the end of it. It felt strange to be a killer, but she wouldn't take the bullets back even if she could.

She moved to the sink and started rinsing the dishes as she stared out the window. It was an unusually drab day by Florida standards, with a gray, gloomy sky pocketed with cirrus clouds. She had little doubt that it would start raining soon. You could practically smell the precipitation hanging in the humid air. Normally, she cracked the window while she did the dishes, but with a storm imminent, she didn't bother.

She sighed, resigned herself to being trapped inside until the rain passed, and reached for the dishwasher handle so she could start stacking the dirty plates.

She heard the front door open, an oil-deprived hinge squeaking ever so slightly.

Shiomi froze. The plate in her hand slipped from

her fingers and clattered back into the sink. Her heartbeat jumped up several notches as her eyes narrowed and her lips tightened. She distinctly remembered locking the door when she came home from her trip to the mall, and nobody but her and Malakai had the key. They didn't even leave a spare one hidden outside.

Another squeak as the door opened further.

She crept over to the wall and peered around the corner at the front door, half-expecting to see a police officer standing in the living room, a detective come to arrest her for killing Nick Caesar down in Miami. Or maybe one of their enemies had tracked them down. After all, Asher and Larissa had been attacked just yesterday.

Multiple possibilities, and none of them gave her any comfort.

The door was wide open, but there was nobody there.

The moist air seeped in from the porch, the smell of rain even stronger now. Thunder rumbled like a warning.

Shiomi quickly scanned the room but didn't see anybody. She hustled over as fast as she could on her prosthetic leg to the front door and pushed it closed, turning the lock as soon as the latch clicked into place. Her heart rate was still elevated, but she was starting to doubt herself.

Maybe I did forget to make sure it was closed behind me, and the wind blew it open. Need to be more careful.

A floorboard creaked behind her.

She turned, fear lending speed to her movements, and came face-to-face with a rigid specter who seemed to materialize out of thin air. The man had not been there a moment before, but now stood just a foot away, dressed in black and sporting an eye patch. His hand shot out like a striking cobra and grabbed her slender neck.

She tried to cry out but was instantly choked into silence. Desperate, she attacked the intruder, kicking and punching and doing everything she could to break his death-grip on her throat. His fingers plunged deep into her milky skin, digging for her windpipe. She could feel it on the verge of collapse and had no doubt he could rip her throat out with very little effort.

Her attacker stared at her, cold and unfazed, his single eye dead of all emotion. Her blows bounced off his hard, statuesque body as if it were sculpted from stone.

She needed air. Needed it desperately. Her panicked body quivered, and her vision blurred, going dark around the edges. Her hands flailed out from her sides, looking for something, anything, that she could grab and smash over the man's head.

But before that could happen, he slammed her sideways into the wall, her head cratering the sheetrock next to a framed picture of a Japanese orchid. He pulled her back and slammed her into the wall again. The third time was enough to take all the fight out of her, leaving her only semi-conscious and limp as a ragdoll in his grasp.

The ruthless intruder refused to release her throat. Vision dark, brain rattled by the repeated blows, she was helpless to defy him. He radiated raw, primeval power, and even at her best, she could not have bested him.

She was dimly aware that it had started raining

heavily outside, the skies opening as if someone had slit the bellies of the clouds. As the droplets hammered the roof, the man made a hushing noise and murmured, "Do not worry. It will all be over soon."

Shiomi felt herself slipping away. She had no way of knowing that the man choking the life from her was named Nakano. No way of knowing for what sins she was being killed, no way of knowing why he had come for her.

All that mattered, the only thing she kept thinking about as the cold, choking darkness rushed up like a black, suffocating tide to claim her, was that she would never see Malakai again.

———

The bullet crease in Asher's head throbbed like hell, but not half as much as the anger that throbbed in his heart. Not hot anger, not the kind that exploded out of control and resulted in foolish, reckless decisions. Rather, this anger was ice cold and laser-focused on taking the fight to the Crimson Cross psychos who had snatched a little girl and now abducted her mother. He had no way of knowing if Amy or Rene were alive, but if they were, he vowed to get them back. And if they weren't, he vowed to avenge their deaths.

They were heading west down Route 17, a two-lane highway that cut through a large portion of New York's southern tier, in a black Dodge Durango borrowed from the FBI office in Elmira. Their headlights punched through the darkness, but dawn was only an hour away. Senator Olander had arranged for the SUV to be delivered to the airport with no questions asked and a small arsenal in the cargo hold, but it had taken the better part of the night to make it all happen.

Asher drove while Malakai checked their weapons. "How the hell did this happen?" Malakai muttered, mostly to himself, but loud enough for Asher to catch the words and the frustration contained within them. It wasn't the first time his friend had voiced the question. It had been a running refrain throughout the night.

"Good question," Asher replied, also not for the first time. He swerved around a slow-moving Prius camped out in the left lane. "But what's done is done."

"Somebody fucked us, and fucked us hard."

"No doubt. But we'll figure out who and why later. Right now, we've got to deal with the sons of bitches who took Amy and Rene."

Asher nodded and started topping off magazines. They had burned through a lot of ammo back at the airport. Their mags needed to be replenished before they hit the farm at dawn and rained hell down on the Crimson Cross thugs. They didn't speak for miles, the comfortable silence that exists between longtime friends. Asher concentrated on getting them to the target zone while Malakai readied their gear so they could hit the ground running when they got there.

They had just passed the exit for the town of Campbell when Malakai's cellphone started ringing. He dug his hand into the cargo pocket of his pants, muttering, "Who the hell is calling me at this ungodly hour?"

"Make it quick," Asher said. "We're only ten minutes out."

Malakai looked at the caller ID. "It's Shiomi."

"Better take it."

Malakai put the phone to his ear. "Hello?"

"Don't talk." A strange male voice on the other end of the connection growled. "Just listen."

"Who is this?" He glanced over at Asher, a puzzled look on his face.

A moment later, he heard Shiomi.

Screaming.

"Shiomi!" Malakai shouted into the phone. "Shiomi, can you hear me?"

"Malakai!" she cried out.

"Hold on, baby. I'm coming for you."

No words, just another scream of pain.

"You fucking piece of shit!" Malakai yelled. "Leave her alone. Talk to me. Who are you? What do you want?"

"You can call me penance for your past sins," the man intoned. "Your beloved girlfriend is in my hands now. If you want to save her, you know what you have to do."

"Just tell me where, you son of a bitch. I'll be there."

"Come home, and we can put an end to this matter like honorable men."

"Not sure how honorable you're gonna feel when I put you down like a fucking dog, asshole."

"Just come home, assassin. Your fate awaits."

The call ended, leaving only chilling, ominous silence where the man's cold, raspy voice had been. Malakai slammed the phone down and let out a primal roar of rage.

"Talk to me," Asher said. "What happened?"

"Somebody came to my house. They've got Shiomi."

"Any idea who they are?"

"Something about paying for the sins of my past."

"Syndicate?"

"Be my best guess."

"What's the plan?"

"I have to go."

"Of course you have to go." Asher hesitated, then added, "But I can't come with you this time."

"I understand," Malakai assured him.

"You sure?"

"Yeah," Malakai replied. "There's a little girl who needs saving."

Asher nodded. "If it were just Rene, I'd leave her to her fate. She's guilty of God knows how many crimes and pretty much deserves whatever happens to her. But that little girl is innocent. I can't turn back and let those Russian pricks have their way with her."

"I get it," Malakai said. "And I agree with you." He pointed at a road sign as it flashed by. "Says there's a rest area a mile ahead. Drop me off there. My fight's back home. Your fight is here."

"I hate letting you fly solo on this one."

"This fight is mine," Malakai said. "This time, I don't want you on my six. I want you to save that little girl."

They pulled into the rest area, and Asher steered the SUV into a parking spot. As Malakai opened the door to disembark, Asher said, "No mercy, brother. Make 'em pay."

"You know it," Malakai replied. "This son of a bitch dared to put his hands on Shiomi and hurt her. No way does he get to keep on living after that." He reached over and slapped his friend on the shoulder. "Sure you're gonna be okay on your own?"

"Been there before. I'll get it done."

"Bury the bastards."

"That's the plan."

"And don't get dead. Larissa would never forgive me."

"I'm not gonna be the one doing the dying today," Asher said grimly.

Malakai nodded and closed the door. No more words, no goodbyes. They went their separate ways, each with their own mission, their own targets, their own fears. Would they see each other again? Neither of them knew for sure, but they didn't dwell on the uncertainty. They had jobs to do, and now was not the time for melancholy musings.

It was time for scorched earth.

CHAPTER 22

ASHER HAD SPENT a lot of years working alone. This was just one more time.

Just like the old days.

He planned to come down on the Crimson Cross hideout like a raging storm.

Olander had checked in shortly after he dropped off Malakai and said their intel indicated that this remote farm was part of the Crimson Cross human trafficking network. They sometimes kept the girls here until they could transport them up to Buffalo, often smuggling them into Canada. Best guess was, the scumbags planned on making Amy and Rene disappear into the vile world of sex slavery, the hideous plan orchestrated by Sammy Quattro as payback for Rene ordering the death of his son.

Asher had no plans on letting that happen.

He felt guilty about leaving Malakai to face whatever fate waited for him down in Florida on his own, but they both lived by a code to protect innocents, and there was no one more innocent than a young child.

Malakai was doing what he absolutely had to do, and Asher was exactly where he needed to be. Wasn't the first time they had split up to accomplish two simultaneous objectives.

He tightened down his Kevlar vest and double-checked the HK45 pistol in its holster, confirming brass bristled in the chamber. He also confirmed the M4 Carbine provided by the FBI contained a full magazine. His Gerber Back Up dagger hung in a sheath opposite the pistol, extra magazines were crammed into every available pocket, and he even had a pair of grenades—one flash-bang, one fragmentation. He was surprised the FBI agent had included them with the weapons cache he had provided when he delivered the Dodge Durango.

He could feel the adrenaline pumping through his system, the fuel he would use to bring hellfire to the kidnappers.

Scorched earth, damn straight.

Time to burn it all down.

He left the SUV hidden behind an old, abandoned one-room schoolhouse on a dirt road and approached the farm from the west as dawn turned the sky from dark to gray. He crossed a patch of ice-dappled brush and dropped down into a wooded ravine with a narrow creek twisting through the bottom. Some of the quieter parts of the stream were still crusted over, but the main channel flowed freely, weaving between tall trees stripped down to skeletal forms by the harsh hand of winter.

He used a fallen log to cross the creek as a crow cawed at him from the upper branches of a poplar tree, and a rabbit was tearing away as if its cotton-ball backside was on fire. He pushed through some saplings and navigated to the top of the opposite slope, doing his best to minimize the sound of the snow crunching beneath his boots.

He found himself greeted by a drooping, rusted barbed wire fence that ran along the edge of an old apple orchard. The stunted fruit trees partially blocked his view of the barn, but he was able to perform a decent enough scan of the area with his binoculars.

It was a traditional style barn, old and dilapidated, roof sagging in the middle like a swaybacked horse, with weather-beaten boards that had been scoured of any color they might have once had. Two silos were stacked on each side, looming over the barn like the towers of a rustic castle. Iron walkways encircled the top of the silos, and Asher could see a guard perched on each one.

He had no way of knowing the enemy headcount, nor did he plan to waste time reconning to determine the number. While he sat here and waited, Rene and Amy could be suffering God knew what. He figured at least six hostiles, but possibly a dozen or more. But the numbers didn't really matter. There could be a hundred of the bastards waiting for him, and he would still press forward. He would face down the devil himself if that's what it took to save the Perellis, especially Amy, from fates worse than death.

The distance from his prone position in the ravine to the silos was approximately one hundred and twenty-five meters. Well within the M4's range and his skill level. Hell, he could almost make that shot blindfolded.

The suppressor threaded onto the carbine kept things quiet when he double-tapped the first guard, drilling a pair of 5.56mm bullets into his head. Before the corpse even finished crumpling down on the walkway, Asher had the second sentry in his sights. Another double tap, another dead bad guy.

He crossed the barbed wire fence and moved swiftly through the rundown apple orchard, needing to close the gap between himself and the barn before anyone noticed the headshot bastards up on the silo walkways. He flitted from tree to tree like a stalking ghost, hating the sound of the snow crackling under his boots but unable to do anything about it. Not even a ninja could have navigated this snow without making noise.

Two more guards emerged from the opposite side of the barn, bundled in heavy coats, clearly on patrol, even though their rifles were slung over their shoulders so that they could keep their hands stuffed in their pockets for warmth like the sloppy amateurs they were.

Asher shot the first goon in the neck, the bullet blowing out the top of his spinal column to drop him in his tracks. The second guy took his bullet in the upper lip, tearing apart the palate on its way to the brain. He hit the ground beside his instantly dead buddy, both of them splattering blood all over the snow in abstract patterns of crimson.

He reached the edge of the orchard and paused, waiting, watching, but didn't see any more roving patrols. He dashed across the frozen ground toward the barn door. There was a lock and chain, but it hung loose. The Crimson Cross probably figured the guards were deterrent enough. Asher wasted no time penetrating the interior.

He went to work with the M4, dropping any Russian he came into contact with. Constantly swiveling, spinning, moving with deadly grace, covering the corners, watching the angles, checking his six. All the junk and detritus stacked haphazardly in the barn turned it into some kind of alien landscape, but he moved through it fluidly and delivered headshots like they were Halloween candy as enemy combatants swarmed out of the shadows.

When the M4's bolt locked open, Asher effortlessly transitioned to the pistol. Another gangster went down with his skull riveted by .45 slugs.

Asher stayed in constant motion, a gunslinging phantom, clipping Crimson Cross motherfuckers as he steadily pushed toward the back of the barn. Chest shots, headshots, gut shots...It didn't matter, as long as the enemy targets went down.

A burst of fire from above sent Asher rolling along the ground, trying to dodge the salvo from the gunner in the hayloft. Bullets tracked toward him, kicking up splinters from the warped floorboards.

Still rolling, he passed the ladder that accessed the loft. Another two rotations, and he was underneath the elevated gunman. Bits of dust and hay trickled down from the cracks in the boards above him to give away the bastard's position.

Asher pumped four rapid shots through the floor of the loft. He heard a cry of pain, the thump of a falling body, and then everything got quiet up there. Instead of dust and hay, blood now streamed through the cracks, hot and thick like maple syrup.

Asher powered back up on his feet and kept moving deeper into the barn.

He reached the back corner less than a minute later and spotted a pair of ancient, rusting tractors sitting on dry-rotted tires, their exposed engines covered with cobwebs. Another Crimson Cross gunner tried to welcome him with a burst of auto-fire, but it flew wide. Asher responded with a burst of his own, popping the target's chest full of holes. As the goon staggered back, face locked in an agonized grimace, Asher drilled a shot through his head to finish him off.

"Hello?"

Asher recognized Rene's voice. He moved forward carefully, scanning for more guards. None showed up, and a moment later, he spotted Rene tied to a post with nylon rope. She was in a sitting position with her legs stretched out in front of her. Blood soaked her leg and shoulder from the bullet wounds she had sustained at the airport. She had clearly been beaten, her usually pretty face now a swollen mask of bruises.

"Hey," he said as he approached.

"Asher?" She strained at him as if she was having difficulty seeing through eyes that were little more than dark slits in punished flesh.

"Yeah." He stepped close, drew his knife, and slashed the ropes binding her to the post. "I thought you were dead."

"Close call with a bullet. Thank God I have a hard head."

"You came for Amy."

"I came for both of you."

Rene just looked at him, as if unsure what to say.

Before she could formulate any words, a Crimson Cross thug materialized, holding a whimpering Amy in front of him as a shield. The little girl looked terrified, but she did not appear to have been beaten like her mother. The tracking device necklace still hung around her neck. Clearly, the Russians had no idea how their location had been found.

The goon pressed a pistol against the little girl's temple. "Drop the gun, motherfucker," he growled, his voice thick with a Russian accent. "Both of them."

Amy whimpered again, the sound soft and pitiful.

Asher hesitated, sizing up the situation, mind racing through options.

"I said, drop them. Won't tell you again. Fuck with me, and the girl gets dead." He screwed the muzzle of the pistol even harder against Amy's head, dimpling the tender flesh. His finger tightened on the trigger, nearing breakpoint.

Amy shuddered, tears streaming down her cheeks.

Silently vowing to do whatever it took to keep her alive, Asher tossed the pistol. "All right, have it your way."

"The rifle too."

Asher shrugged off the M4. It fell to the barn floor.

"Let her go," Rene pleaded. "We can work this out. I have money. You can have it. All of it. Just let my baby go."

"We've already been paid a lot of money by Sammy Quattro."

"I can pay you more."

"Fuck you, whore. That's not the way this works. I'm not negotiating with you."

"She's a child, for god's sake!"

"Which means she'll fetch a good price. You should have thought about all of this before you killed Mr. Quattro's son."

"Please, let her go. Take me instead."

The Russian shook his head. "You made the son pay

for the sins of the father, so now your daughter must pay for the sins of her mother."

"Anyone touches her, I won't just kill them. I'll cut them into a thousand pieces first."

"Tough words from a woman who's been shot twice and beaten like a back talking bitch." The Crimson Cross scumbag looked at Asher. "You have any more weapons on you?"

"Yeah, actually." Asher pulled a fragmentation grenade from his pocket and whipped it through the air at the guy. "Catch, asshole."

The man's eyes widened as the explosive rocketed toward him like a line-drive baseball, too fast for him to realize that the pin was still inserted. Thinking he was about to die in a razor storm of shrapnel, he shoved Amy away as he scrambled for safety.

Asher scooped up his .45 and fired two shots at the fleeing target. The first one caught him just above the waist and severed his spine. The second one punched into the back of the skull and blew apart his face on the way out.

The grenade dropped harmlessly to the floor and rolled to a stop between the dead man's twitching legs.

Amy scrambled over to her mother, sobbing. Rene wrapped her good arm around her daughter and squeezed like she would never let go again. The other arm hung uselessly at her side, her shoulder a mess of torn tissue and coagulated blood.

"It's okay, baby. Mommy's here. I've got you."

Asher quickly swept the rest of the barn, making sure it was clear of Crimson Cross thugs. When he returned, Rene was still clutching her daughter tight.

"I hate to interrupt the reunion," he said. "But we can't hang around here very long."

Rene nodded, let go of Amy, and held out her hand. Asher took it and helped her to her feet. She could barely stand on her injured leg. She winced, then gritted her teeth and took the pain.

"Sammy Quattro has to die," she said. "Until he's gone, Amy won't be safe."

Asher nodded. "I know."

"That bastard is going to find out he fucked with the wrong family."

"Mommy," Amy said, "that's bad language."

Rene smiled at her daughter. "Sorry, honey." Then she looked back at Asher, and the smile evaporated. "You killed my husband," she said flatly. "I know in the game we play, death is always a possibility, and you were just doing your job, but that doesn't change the fact that you killed him right in front of me and my daughter."

"I know what I did," said Asher. "And if I could take it back, I would."

"But you can't," Rene replied. "Just like I can never forgive you for doing it."

"Not sure this is the time to hash out old wounds," Asher said. "If any of these guys called for backup before I dropped them, there could be reinforcements inbound. We need to haul ass before things get real hot again."

"I'm not trying to open old wounds," Rene said. "I'm trying to say that it's over."

"What's over?"

"Our feud. The bad blood between us. Not because you saved me, but because you saved *her*. You saved my daughter, the only thing in my life that matters. And for that, it's over. I owe you that much."

"You don't owe me anything," Asher replied. "If anything, I owe you for what I took from you."

"And that's why I can't give you forgiveness," Rene said. "I loved my husband too much to ever forgive you for taking him away from us. All I can offer is the promise that it's behind us."

"I'll take it."

"Good," she said. "Now let's get the hell out of here."

CHAPTER 23

BY THE TIME Malakai reached his house in Florida—courtesy of a private jet ride arranged by Olander—it was mid-morning, and his worry for Shiomi had skyrocketed to unbearable levels. He circled the house, trying to see through the windows to gauge what awaited him inside, but all the blinds had been lowered.

Stealth and caution be damned. It was time to breach.

He rushed up the back steps and barreled through the door.

"Shiomi!"

No answer. Nothing but silence greeted his call. With the blinds drawn, the house was dim and full of shadows.

He moved through the house like he was clearing an enemy stronghold. When he reached the living room, he spotted someone sitting in his favorite recliner in front of the fireplace. Someone else was sprawled on the floor at the stranger's feet. Malakai narrowed his eyes, assessing the outlines, trying to decipher the shadow-shapes. He kept his FNX-45 pistol trained on the person in the chair with one hand while his other hand reached for the light switch on the wall.

The illumination revealed a tall man sitting there, facing him, leaning forward slightly, one eye covered by a patch, exuding all the confidence in the world. He seemed unfazed by the gun muzzle pointed at his head.

Probably because Shiomi lay at his feet, bound and trussed with duct tape like a hog for slaughter, and he had the barrel of a stainless steel .357 Magnum revolver shoved in her mouth with the hammer cocked. Her prosthetic leg had been removed and tossed into the corner, making it nearly impossible for her to escape, even if she somehow managed to thrash free of the duct tape.

Malakai moved into the room and wasted no time getting to the point. "Let her go."

"Four pounds of pressure," the man replied. "That is all it will take for the hammer to drop and turn Shiomi's skull into a jigsaw puzzle. I strongly suggest you do not make any wrong moves if you wish to prevent that from happening."

"You got a name?" Malakai asked.

"Call me Nakano."

"I've heard of you."

"As I have heard of you."

Malakai took his eyes off the Japanese assassin long enough to glance down at Shiomi. Her eyes pleaded with him for rescue, for salvation, for an end to the fear and misery. But with the cocked gun in her mouth, there was little he could do. Even shooting Nakano in the head would result in a death spasm that might clench his finger against the trigger and blow Shiomi's brains out. He could try to shoot the finger instead—he had done it before, when Shiomi's father had put a gun to her head—but the angle was all wrong, the revolver's cylinder blocking all but a sliver of knuckle.

She wasn't dead yet, and while there was life, there was hope, so he decided to let it play out.

"What do you want?" Malakai asked, pistol still raised. Given the slightest opportunity, he wouldn't hesitate to shoot. He just needed that Magnum barrel out of Shiomi's mouth.

As if sensing his thoughts, Nakano shoved the barrel in even deeper. Malakai winced at the sound of metal scraping against teeth, the horrible gagging sound Shiomi made.

He stepped forward, ready to lunge. "You motherfucker."

"Move another inch and I will put a bullet down her throat," Nakano warned.

Malakai stayed where he was. He wanted to strike out, make a move, do something, anything, to end the standoff. But there was nothing he could do that wouldn't get Shiomi killed. So he stood still and asked again, "What do you want?"

"It is not what I want," Nakano replied. "It is what the Syndicate wants. And what the Syndicate wants is your life, followed by hers."

"Take me and leave her alone. I won't even fight you. How's that for a deal?"

"But you see, I *want* you to fight me."

"Why?"

"Because some would say I am the best assassin in the world, others would say you are. Time to put it to the test and discover the truth."

"Actually," Malakai said, "Asher is the best."

Nakano cocked his head in a *maybe, maybe not* motion. "Debatable," he said. "But since Asher is not here at the moment, I am content to pit my skills against yours."

Malakai stared at him for a moment, then shrugged. "What the hell."

He ejected the magazine from his pistol. It dropped on the carpet at his feet, and he kicked it under the couch. He then racked the slide, ejecting the cartridge in the chamber before tossing the gun across the room. "If it's a fight you want, asshole, then let's stop fucking around and get down to business."

Nakano moved with a speed that bordered on the supernatural. Malakai was caught completely off guard as the Syndicate assassin erupted from the chair and fired off a blistering flurry of kicks and punches that drove Malakai backward. But at least the .357 Magnum was no longer in Shiomi's mouth.

Time to kill this son of a bitch.

Turned out that was easier said than done.

Before he could gather himself, another kick thundered into his ribs, knocking him sideways. A left hook came out of nowhere to detonate against his chin. He staggered again, off balance, flank and face flushed with pain.

Steel flashed as Nakano tried to hammer the barrel of the revolver into the side of his skull, hoping to either knock him out or crack bone. Malakai managed to mostly deflect the strike with a defensive sweep so that the barrel only grazed the top of his head. No real damage, just enough to sting.

Malakai snarled a curse and struck back with a

savage jab to the solar plexus that elicited a grunt from Nakano. He followed up with a right hook to the face that would have broken Nakano's jaw, but the assassin turned his head at the last possible microsecond, and Malakai's knuckles merely brushed him instead of breaking bone. He managed to chop down with the same hand and knock the gun out of Nakano's grasp.

The two men battled back and forth, from one end of the living room to the other, trashing the place as they traded blows. Malakai knew he was taking more shots than he was giving. Nakano might be a stone-cold prick, but he was a hell of a fighter. Even if he survived this fight, Malakai knew he would be a black and blue mess.

The conflict moved out of the totaled living room and into the kitchen. Malakai whipped dishes at Nakano, glass and ceramic shattering like shrapnel. A well-aimed coffee mug crashed into Nakano's mouth, pulping his lips against his teeth. The Syndicate assassin spat blood and enamel chips and then grabbed a butcher blade from the knife set on the counter.

"Had enough of the bare hands shit, huh?" Malakai said. "Okay, fine." He yanked open a drawer and pulled out a meat cleaver that looked big enough to decapitate Godzilla. "We'll do this dance your way."

"You are a worthy adversary," Nakano intoned solemnly, almost respectfully, blood dripping from his crushed lips. "Perhaps even better than I anticipated. But you talk too much."

"Just waiting for you, asshole."

Nakano twirled the knife in his fingers, the honed steel spinning so fast it looked like the rotor blades on a chopper.

"Come on," Malakai rasped, his voice sharp and fiery, betraying no evidence of the pain he felt all over his battered body. "Bring it."

"Time for you to die." Nakano slashed forward with the butcher knife.

Metal clashed against metal as Malakai blocked the strike with his meat cleaver. Nakano immediately lowered the blade and attempted another slash, but Malakai pivoted out of the way and chopped at the assassin's chest. Only Nakano's cobra-fast reflexes saved him from getting his sternum carved open by the cleaver.

Malakai swung again, missing Nakano's face by less than an inch.

So close.

But close wasn't good enough in this deadly game.

Nakano's hand whipped out. Malakai tried to dodge out of the way, but the butcher knife caught him low, slicing through his shirt and leaving a thin red line across his abdomen. The shallow cut burned as it wept blood, but Malakai ignored it. He'd had worse shaving nicks.

Nakano attacked again, a fast, stabbing thrust designed to skewer. Malakai knocked the knife aside with the cleaver. Nakano bulled forward and crashed his shoulder into Malakai's chest, pushing him back until his spine jarred up against the ridge of the counter.

As he gritted his teeth against the pain, Malakai glanced over Nakano's lowered shoulder and saw Shiomi struggling on the living room floor, trying desperately to free herself. She thrashed furiously against her bonds, but the duct tape refused to give.

Pressed against the counter by Nakano's bulk, Malakai sensed the other assassin trying to get the knife into position to stab him in the back of the neck. He powered his knee up, sharp and quick, going for Nakano's balls. Nakano twisted away, and Malakai fired a kick into the man's right kneecap. The leg buckled slightly, and Malakai seized the opportunity to slash the cleaver at Nakano's neck, hoping to chop the bastard's head right off or at least sever the carotid artery. He would happily crack open a beer and watch the fucker bleed out.

But Nakano recovered from the knee strike and ducked below the chop. As the cleaver whiffed over his head like a baseball batter striking out, he stuck the butcher blade into Malakai's thigh and gave it a quick twist, tearing open the meat. Malakai snarled a curse and retreated, waving the cleaver like a mad chef to keep Nakano from pressing his advantage. Blood streamed down his leg.

Nakano lunged forward, sensing victory. Malakai spun to the side and slashed with the cleaver. The edge scored a gash across Nakano's ribcage and the assassin hissed in pain.

"Blood for blood," Malakai rasped.

Nakano did not respond. Just lashed out with the knife. Malakai parried the blow and then managed to rake the edge of the cleaver up the man's right arm, laying him open from wrist to elbow. Nerves, veins, and tendons severed, Nakano's fingers spasmed open, and the butcher blade clattered to the kitchen floor.

But he wasn't out of the fight yet.

The Syndicate assassin powered forward into another attack. A straight left hook shot out like a piston and pummeled Malakai on the chin. As he fell back, Malakai managed to snare Nakano's wrist with his left hand and jerk him forward, off balance.

His right hand swung the meat cleaver right into the motherfucker's face.

The heavy blade sank into Nakano's forehead with a sickening crunch and split his skull open like an over-ripe watermelon. Blood and brain matter burst from the gaping wound and oozed down his shocked face. Nakano fell at Malakai's feet, dead before his bisected head hit the floor.

Malakai left the meat cleaver buried in the man's cranium, grabbed the fallen butcher knife, and hobbled back into the living room. Pain from the punches, cuts, and stabbings he had endured made him clench his jaw, but it was nothing he couldn't handle, and a whole lot better than being in Nakano's position right now.

He kneeled down beside Shiomi, cut away the duct tape, and pulled her close. "I've got you," he said. "I've got you."

She clutched at him. "I thought he was going to kill you."

"He gave it his best shot."

"The Syndicate will just send someone else, you know." She sounded hopeless, defeated, nothing like the spunky, spirited woman he had fallen in love with. "They'll never stop hunting us."

"They should have left us alone," Malakai said. "Because now I'm going to chop off the head of the snake."

Shiomi leaned her head against his chest. "You'd have to find him first."

"I'll find him."

They stayed like that for a while, content to just sit on the floor in the middle of a battle-trashed living room and hold each other. Malakai knew he would need to call the Church and report all this so a cleanup crew could be dispatched, but that could wait. He had come dangerously close to losing Shiomi, a thought that chilled him to the quick, and right now he felt like he could never let go of her. The way her arms gripped him tight, she seemed to feel the same.

"Thanks for saving my ass again," she said.

"I'll always be here for you," Malakai replied. "Never doubt that. I'll kill anyone who gets in my way."

"Sometimes it seems like our lives are nothing but a bunch of blood and bullets."

Malakai smiled. "Now you're starting to sound like Gabriel."

"Think it'll ever change?"

"God only knows."

CHAPTER 24

ASHER RETURNED Rene and Amy Perelli safely back to their hilltop estate in Hartford and then headed down to Greystone on Hudson to drop the curtain on Samuel 'Saigon Sammy' Quattro once and for all. Not only did the old mobster deserve it on general principles, but he had ordered the abduction, trafficking, and eventual slaughter of a little girl. Asher had no tolerance for those who targeted and preyed on innocents.

Yeah, Rene had ordered the execution of Sammy's son, but Taide had been an adult and heavily involved in his father's illicit empire. Taide had willingly played the game, had understood the cutthroat rules, and had justifiably paid the price. He had not been an innocent, not by a long shot.

Plus, all signs indicated that Quattro had orchestrated the assault on Asher and Larissa's house in Keene Valley. Asher was not the kind of person to let that kind of transgression stand. Time to put the old son of a bitch down and let his criminal empire get dismantled.

He infiltrated the mansion with minimal effort, in

full-throttle obliteration mode. He stormed room to room, gunned down all resistance, and left a trail of the dead in his wake. Quattro's security forces might have been hot shit in the mob world, but they were woefully inadequate against someone like Asher. Bullets tore them apart like they were blood-filled piñatas getting smashed by a wrecking ball.

No hesitation, no mercy. It was a slaughter.

Asher found Sammy Quattro in his suite, sitting on the edge of his bed. He made no move to defend himself as Asher entered the room, seemingly accepting of his fate, as if he had always known it would come down to this.

"My men?" the crime boss asked.

"Dead down to the last man."

"You butchered them."

"Call it what you will. Your actions put them in my gunsights."

"That Perelli whore started this vendetta when she killed my son."

"You got into bed with the Crimson Cross," Asher replied. "And then you lost control of them. You know the rules of the game, you know how this shit works. But I wouldn't be standing here if you and Perelli had been content to take each other out. Your mistake was attacking my home and then targeting a little kid. *That's* what brought me to your doorstep."

"That attack wasn't meant to kill you. It was meant to goad you into taking out Perelli."

"Seems your boys got a little overzealous. They hit us with an RPG and were definitely in shoot-to-kill mode."

Quattro shrugged. "Those useless dipshits?

Nothing but cannon fodder. All part of the ruse. I didn't doubt for a single second that a man of your skill and reputation would put them all down."

"How'd you figure out where I live?"

"It pays to have friends in high places."

"I'll bet it does," Asher said. "But whoever those friends are, they can't help you now. Even if I was willing to overlook your stupidity on attacking my house, I'm not willing to stand for what you did to that little girl."

Quattro nodded. "Yeah, I kind of figured you might come hunting once I heard you were involved."

"The hunt's over." Asher raised the HK45.

Quattro shrugged again. "I had a good run." He grinned broadly, flashing Asher an unrepentant smile, not an ounce of remorse on his timeworn face. "So what are you waiting for? You came here to kill me, so get on with it, you bastard. I've got a dinner date with the devil."

Sammy Quattro deserved a hard death, given everything he had done in his wicked lifetime, but Asher let him off easy. A simple pull of the trigger, and the pistol bucked in his hand. Quattro's head snapped back with a bloody entry hole between his eyes. The exit wound in the back of his head was much larger.

Asher didn't waste time spitting a quip at the dead man. He stepped past the corpse and retrieved the mobster's cell phone from the nightstand. He would deliver it to the Church, and Vesper or Wyatt could strip it for intel. God only knew what juicy secrets they might find on the device. Maybe it would lead them to the mole in their ranks.

Asher took out his own cell phone and made a call.

Rene Perelli answered. "Is it done?"

"It's done," Asher confirmed. "He's in hell, paying for his sins."

"Thank you."

"I didn't do it just for you. I had my own reasons."

"I understand. You have your own sins to pay for. But I'll leave that to God."

"I can't take it back, Rene. I can't give you back the husband I took from you, the father I took from Amy. But just know that if I could, I would."

"I believe you," Rene replied. "I just can't forgive you."

"I don't expect you to."

"You and I, we're done," Rene said. A slight pause, then she added, "Goodbye, Gabriel."

Asher almost replied, *See you around*, but then thought better of it. Instead, he simply mirrored her own words.

"Goodbye, Rene."

CHAPTER 25

WHEN ASHER GOT BACK to the Church, Senator Olander was there. He handed her the cell phone he had retrieved from Quattro's residence.

Olander's eyes narrowed. "What's this?"

Asher couldn't help himself. "It's a phone."

"Don't be a smartass. That's Malakai's job."

"It's Sammy Quattro's."

"How'd you manage to get your hands on it?"

"Killed him."

"I didn't sanction that."

"I didn't ask for your permission."

Olander's lips tightened. "You need a refresher on how things work around here."

"And you need to remember that I'm not your pet dog."

Olander gave him a steely stare, then turned to Vesper, who was sitting at her desk watching the tense exchange. The senator handed the pretty young analyst the phone. "Unlock this, please."

"Yes, ma'am." Vesper connected the cell phone to her computer, performed some kind of hacker voodoo magic trick, and less than ninety seconds later, handed it back to Olander. "There you go."

Asher watched as Olander scrolled through the phone. He couldn't see what she was looking at, but a few moments later, her eyes popped wide open. "Holy shit."

"What is it?"

"That arrogant, goddamned, dirty little snake." She turned the phone over and showed him the screen, open to Quattro's contacts. "Recognize that number?"

Asher shook his head. "No."

"That's the personal cell phone number for Vice President John Steinbeck."

"Quattro has the VP in his back pocket?"

"That's what I'm going to find out."

———

Olander stormed through the West Wing of the White House like a woman on a mission. Her lips were a thin, bloodless slash across her face, and her eyes flashed dangerous fire that made people move out of her way.

She didn't actually kick open the door to the vice president's office, but she entered the room with so much angry, forceful energy that it had the same effect. Dressed in a sharp navy suit, Steinbeck stood in front of his desk with two other Washington sycophants bracing him on either side. He looked at her in surprise when she barged in.

"Paula? I wasn't expecting you."

I wonder how long it will take to break him, Olander thought. Aloud, she said, "I know you weren't."

The VP's eyes narrowed. "Not sure I care for your tone."

"You're going to like what I have to say even less." Her eyes flicked to the men at his side, who both clearly looked uncomfortable. "You should probably tell your bootlickers that they're dismissed before we get down to business." She made damn sure it sounded like an order, not a suggestion.

Steinbeck clearly did not like being talked to that way, as evidenced by his frown of displeasure. But he put his hands on the shoulder of each man and gently nudged them toward the door. "Gentlemen, if you don't mind, please excuse us. I'm sure this won't take long."

"Don't bother waiting," Olander said to the two men as they exited the office and closed the door behind them.

Steinbeck glared at her, arms folded across his chest in what he probably assumed was a power stance. "So, Paula, you mind telling me what you're doing here?"

"You were playing a dangerous game, John, and you got caught."

"I have no idea what you're talking about."

"Oh, I think you do."

"Now who's the one playing games?" Steinbeck growled. "You think I know something? Then go ahead and spell it out for me. Beating around the bush was never your style."

"Fine," Olander said. "Sammy Quattro is dead, we have his phone, and your personal number is in it."

"I have no idea how he would have gotten that."

"Have some dignity and spare me the bullshit lies," Olander retorted. "We know you gave it to him."

"You only *think* you know," Steinbeck said. "But you don't know *shit*."

"Oh, we know. Trust me, John—we know."

"I want you to stop and think very carefully about the ground you're treading on, Paula. The accusation you're making against *the fucking vice president* of the United States. Think about the consequences."

Olander remained stone-faced. "The only one who should be thinking about consequences is you, Mr. Fucking Vice President. The gig is up."

Steinbeck shook his head, as if he couldn't believe what he was hearing. "God, you're such a stupid twat, you know that?"

"We found your accounts in the Cayman Islands and Belize. I've got cold, hard proof that you've received millions of dollars from the Quattro crime family."

Steinbeck uncrossed his arms and let them hang by his side, fists clenched. "So you got me dead to rights. What's your next move, Senator?"

"No denial? No begging and pleading with me to understand that I've got it all wrong?"

"Not really the begging and pleading type, Paula. You know that."

"Don't you have any shame? Any remorse?"

"What I have is a hell of a lot of money."

"Are you seriously telling me there wasn't enough dirty money in politics for you?"

"This was a whole lot easier than sucking up to lobbyists."

"Yeah, well, all your easy money is gone," Olander said. "We hacked the accounts and transferred it all into a black bag slush fund. The assassination game isn't cheap, you know, and the government thanks you for your contribution."

Steinbeck gritted his teeth. "Who the fuck do you think you are?"

"I'm the one who's got you by the balls."

"So that's the play? Squeeze me for something? Just tell me what the hell you want."

"What I want is to have Asher put a bullet in your head," Olander said. "You've committed treason, John."

"That's a stretch, and you know it. Wouldn't have a chance in hell of holding up in court."

Olander smiled coldly. "You might be right, but in case you forgot, Black Talon doesn't bother with the courts."

"So I'm a target now, is that it? You're going to have one of your pet psychos execute a kill order on the vice president of the United States? Is that what you and your little wet work program have come to?" Steinbeck shook his head and snorted derisively. "I should have let Brody Anderson go to the press and burn Black Talon to the ground and danced on the ashes. Instead, I put a muzzle on him, kept him under wraps, and tried to minimize any damage he could do. And this is the thanks I get? A kill threat from the very people I worked my ass off to save?"

"What's sad is that despite all his protests and moral objections, Anderson showed more loyalty to the program than you did," Olander replied. "Listen, I have no intention of having you killed. This country is already a tinderbox ready to explode, and it certainly doesn't need the scandal of an assassinated vice president. Not to mention, we don't want a bunch of Justice

Department law dogs sniffing around our business. So as long as you do what I tell you to do, you'll stay alive and out of prison."

"I'm not going to be a VP that plays lapdog for a senator."

"You're not going to be VP at all," Olander retorted. "I may not have you killed, but I'm sure as hell not going to let a traitor like you stay in power. But we'll get to that. First, I want the name of your source inside Black Talon. Quattro paid you for secrets, and you got them from somebody. I want to know who the goddamned mole is."

"Oh, I'll just bet you do," said Steinbeck. "But what if I tell you to go fuck yourself, Paula?"

"Good question. What if I change my mind about that kill order and have Asher put a bullet in you?"

"He'd have to go through my Secret Service detail, and since they're innocent, he won't do that. Violates that precious little prayer of his."

"Asher could take out your detail using non-lethal methods, and you know it. If I tell him to bring me your head, you're as good as dead. Stop acting like this is your first rodeo and give me the name."

"Fine, have it your way. No reason for me to protect her. She was nothing but a piece of tail, anyway." Steinbeck sighed. "It's Vesper, that pretty little analyst you got at the Church."

Olander felt her heart sink. Vesper? Really? She would have bet her bottom dollar that Wyatt was the one who betrayed them, given his ill-disguised dislike of Asher. She never would have suspected that Vesper would do anything that put Asher and Malakai in harm's way. She knew Asher in particular would take the news hard. He really liked the perky young analyst.

Why, Vesper? Why did you do this to us?

Steinbeck was still talking. "Vesper hooked me up with all the info I needed to share with Quattro. Anytime I needed something, I just gave her a call. Honestly, Paula, when I got in bed with Quattro, I never expected it to come to this."

"You're seventeen kinds of a damn fool, John. What kind of idiot receives millions from the mob and doesn't think they'll have to deliver at some point?"

"I guess I just didn't think it all the way through."

"I think you thought it all the way through perfectly fine and just didn't give a crap," Olander snapped. "You're done. So fucking done. You've only got one choice left to make."

"And what's that?"

"You can go to prison and rot in a cell for the rest of your life while the whole world learns that you're a traitor to your country."

"Or?"

"Or you can hand in your resignation first thing tomorrow morning. I want it on the president's desk before he's had his coffee and bagel."

"You expect me to resign?"

"It's resignation or prison." Olander shrugged. "Like I said, your choice."

"Damn, I think I would have preferred the bullet."

"That can still be arranged."

"Fuck you, Paula." Steinbeck scowled fiercely. "Fuck you right to hell."

"I'm letting you walk away, John," Olander replied,

reaching for the doorknob. "It's a whole lot better than you deserve."

"How do I know you'll let it end there?" he asked as she opened the door.

She gave him a cold smile and a shrug. "You don't. Guess you'll just have to trust that my code of honor is better than yours."

She closed the door behind her as she walked out.

CHAPTER 26

BACK AT THE CHURCH, Olander and Asher summoned Vesper into the conference room. Time to confront the web of lies and deceit that had managed to weave itself right under their noses.

Asher had recovered from the shock of hearing who the mole was, but the sense of betrayal burned deep in his heart. He couldn't believe she had done this to them. When she stepped into the room, he couldn't keep the pain from showing on his face or coming through in his voice.

"Vesper."

Just saying her name hurt. He didn't love her—that was reserved only for Larissa—but he did care for her, and now he had to face the fact that she had provided information for the ambush, sold him out, helped killers find his house, and put him in the line of fire. He felt bile searing his throat and swallowed hard.

Olander brusquely cut right to the chase as soon as Vesper sat down. "We know it was you."

Vesper looked like a student called to the principal's

office, unsure of why she was there, but knowing that it couldn't be good. "I'm sorry, I don't—"

"Let me stop you right there," Olander said, cutting her off, "and save you the time and energy of trying to come up with lame excuses or attempts at deflection. Because Steinbeck gave you up, told us everything."

"I'm not sure I follow."

Asher slapped the table, loud and hard, making the analyst jump in her chair. "Cut the crap, Vesper. I'm not in the mood for it."

Vesper's cheeks turned red. She gnawed at her lower lip as her worried eyes flicked back and forth between Olander and Asher. Her foot tapped the floor in a nervous rhythm, but she didn't say anything.

"The only thing I want to hear out of your mouth," Olander said, "is the reason why you hurt us. I know you're a smart girl, so stop wasting time trying to figure out an exit strategy on this and just come clean."

Vesper's eyes settled on Asher, and a sob burst from her throat as tears spilled down her face. "I'm sorry," she said. "I'm so, so sorry, Gabriel."

Asher just stared at her.

"I'm sorry," she repeated, swiping the back of her hand across her nose. Her wet eyes stayed locked onto Asher as if he were some kind of lifeline or salvation. "I didn't...I just...""I don't want to hear any worthless apology," Olander snapped. "I want to hear a reason why."

The analyst stared at Asher hopelessly.

"Tell me why, Vesper," he said. "Make it make some kind of sense."

"Because..." Her voice trailed off.

Olander snorted. "'Because' isn't an answer, young lady."

Asher leaned forward. "Out with it, Vesper. *Now*."

Vesper took a deep breath and blurted, "I did it because I loved him."

Olander's eyebrows arched. "Excuse me?"

Asher felt his coldness soften ever so slightly. Not much, but a fragment of warmth returned to his eyes when he looked at the analyst. He knew damn well that love could make a person do just about anything. It didn't excuse her betrayal, but it made it more understandable. Steinbeck had sold them out in the name of greed. Vesper had done it for a higher reason, however misguided.

"I loved him," she repeated. "We were...you know, together."

"An affair," Olander clarified. "You were fucking the vice president of the United States."

Vesper shook her head. "No, it was more than that. Something special. At least, I thought it was."

"You wanted it to be," Olander said. "So you played it up that way in your mind until you believed the delusion. Meanwhile, all he was doing was using you. Hell, he literally told me you were nothing but a piece of ass to him."

Vesper lowered her head and dripped tears on the table, trembling slightly, her shame and heartbreak and regret palpable. Asher's anger subsided even more as he felt something close to pity. *Love makes fools of us all,* he thought.

When Vesper raised her head and brushed away the tears, she said, "I guess I got played by an asshole."

"Who initiated, you or him?" Olander asked.

"He made the first move."

"When did it start? How long have you been feeding him intel?"

"We started sleeping together about six months ago. Not long after, he started asking me for information."

Asher asked, "Pretty sure I already know the answer, but did you have anything to do with the attack on my house a few days ago?"

She nodded, and fresh tears slid down her cheeks. "I doctored the DMV records to make it look like the SUV was registered to Rene Perelli."

"Steinbeck ask you to do that?"

Another nod.

Asher clenched his jaw, grinding his teeth together. Yeah, he understood that love made you do stupid things, but those stupid things she had done nearly got him and Larissa killed.

"I'm sorry, Gabriel," she said. "I hate myself more than you know."

"If it makes you feel any better, I kind of hate you right now too."

"Please don't say that," she begged. "Please, whatever you're going to do to me, just do it. But please don't hate me."

"Why wouldn't he?" Olander asked. "He was your friend, and you stabbed him in the back." Without waiting for an answer, the clearly pissed off senator asked another question. "How about the ambush at the airport? You leak that to him?"

"Yes and no," Vesper replied. "He asked me to keep him in the loop on anything related to Sammy Quattro and the Crimson Cross, so I told him what airport Gabe and Malakai were flying into. But I swear I didn't know about the ambush."

"Oh, spare me," Olander snapped. "Bottom line is, you betrayed us, nearly got our guys killed, threw away everything you have, and all for what? Some deep dicking."

"No," Asher said. "She didn't do it for lust. She did it for love."

Olander gave him a look. "You can buy that bullshit if you want, but I don't give two good goddamns why she did it. There are consequences for betraying friends, for betraying this program, for betraying your *country.*" She fixed her gaze on Vesper. "Care to tell me what those consequences are?"

"Death," Vesper replied, her voice cracking.

"You're absolutely right," Olander said. "We're a covert, black ops assassination unit. The penalty for screwing us over is a cheap pine box, six feet deep. You knew that when you came on board."

"I understand." Vesper looked at Asher with tears in her eyes. "I want it to be you."

Asher furrowed his brow. "What do you mean?"

"I want it to be your hand that pulls the trigger. If I have to die, I want you to be the one who does it."

Olander gave him a look that seemed to say, *Your call.*

Asher knew there was no way in hell he could put a bullet in Vesper. She hadn't betrayed them for nefarious reasons. She might be a Judas, but she wasn't interested in a bag full of silver. Her motivation, however misplaced and misguided, was simply a matter of the heart.

She fell in love with a man, and he had twisted that love for his own gains and power. Her desire, her craving to be loved in return, had compelled her to act recklessly, impulsively, without thought for the ramifications of her actions. That was the reality of the situation.

Love made people stupid sometimes.

And while betraying people he cared about wasn't part of who he was, Asher couldn't deny he'd done plenty of so-called dirty deeds in his life. Hypocrisy was one of his pet peeves, and he was in no mood to throw stones at a young woman who had done something terrible because she fell in love with a bad, manipulative man.

No, an execution wasn't in the cards in this case.

"Negative," he said. "I'm not going to kill you."

Vesper gasped with relief. Her tearful eyes glistened with shame, regret, and gratitude. "Thank you," she said simply.

Olander looked like she seriously questioned his decision, but pursed her lips and rolled with it. "Listen up, young lady," she said. "You may have avoided a bullet to the back of the head, but you're not walking away without consequences."

"Believe me, I didn't think I was."

"You're off the team, obviously. Effective immediately, you are no longer part of Black Talon."

"Of course." Vesper still looked like a death row prisoner given a last-minute stay of execution.

"And I want you to leave the country. I don't care where, just as long as it's not here. You've forfeited the right to call this country home."

Vesper clearly didn't like it, but was also smart enough to realize she didn't have a choice. "Okay."

Olander leaned forward, face hard, eyes cold. "And make no mistake, Vesper, if we hear even a whiff that you're talking about Talon, spilling our secrets, then I'll throw every last shred of mercy out the window and hunt you down. Do you understand what I'm telling you?"

Vesper nodded. "I understand."

"I hope so. Now go make a new life for yourself, far away from here, and develop amnesia about your time here. But remember, we will never forget about *you*. You dodged a bullet today, literally, but you're going to spend the rest of your life in the crosshairs. If you become a problem, if you make us regret letting you walk away, then we'll pull the trigger, and you'll never see it coming."

"You won't regret it," Vesper said. "I'll disappear and lie low. I promise."

"You'd damn well better. Now get the fuck out of my sight."

Vesper pushed back her chair and stood up. She faced Asher like she wanted to move toward him, maybe for a goodbye hug or at least a handshake, but seemed uncertain.

"Don't," he said tersely. "Just...don't. Go rebuild your life and forget you ever knew me."

She stared at him, the hurt plain on her face, and another tear chased the others down her cheek. Just one tear, maybe the final one, and then she turned and walked out the door for the last time.

CHAPTER 27

THREE DAYS LATER...

ASHER AND MALAKAI hit Japan and delivered a bloodbath to the Syndicate that the criminal organization would remember for years, maybe even decades, to come. Though battered and bruised, Malakai had vowed to strike back at the evil overlord who had dared to dispatch the killer Nakano to terminate him and Shiomi.

"The son of a bitch has to die," he had growled. "He doesn't get to keep breathing after what he did."

Asher had agreed wholeheartedly. They should have taken out Xiang Fukuda a long time ago instead of putting him on a back burner. This reckoning was long overdue.

They disembarked from the plane, secured the weapons from the prearranged location, and then raided Fukuda's estate.

No quarter, no mercy.

They blazed their way forward with full-auto firepower. The Syndicate soldiers defending the grounds were simply outmatched. Malakai and Asher decimated their ranks like buzz saws ripping through rice paper, the targets toppling like blood-spurting bowling pins. The loyal henchmen died willingly for their master, but they died hard.

Once they breached the interior of the *minka*, the mansion, Asher and Malakai transitioned to pistols, slinging the submachine guns behind their backs. More Syndicate minions appeared, and more Syndicate minions died. The two assassins were simply faster on the trigger, more accurate, more ruthless. They stepped over bloody, twitching corpses and kept on moving.

They found Fukuda and his primary bodyguards in a large room with a waterfall and exotic plants. The *kumicho*, the head of the Syndicate, watched impassively from behind his massive desk as the two assassins tore through his protectors, dropping them as easily as shooting rubber ducks at a carnival.

Fukuda folded his hands in front of him, accepting his fate. Clearly, the gods had willed that his life end here, today. He would not resist.

Malakai stepped forward and looked the bastard dead in the eye. "You know who I am?"

Fukuda nodded. "You have bested *ishinokanbase no kami?*"

"I have no idea what the hell that means."

"Nakano, the stone-faced god."

"That asshole was no god," Malakai said. "He was just a flesh-and-blood man, and he died like one."

"I trust he died with honor."

"He died with a fucking meat cleaver in his face,"

Malakai replied. "You never should have sent him. You should have just left us alone."

"Perhaps," Fukuda acknowledged. "But I am bound by the laws of the life I chose." He bowed his head. "Please make it quick."

"You don't deserve quick," Malakai rasped. "But as long as you're dead, I don't really care."

He shot Fukuda four times.

A bullet in the throat, two to the chest, one to the head.

He didn't linger to gloat over his handiwork. Just holstered his pistol, turned to Asher, and said, "Let's go home."

———

SIX MONTHS LATER...

Former Vice President John Steinbeck had managed to resign from public office with minimal disgrace. Speculation abounded, but he had steadfastly refused to provide the media vultures with any juicy carrion on which to feed. Speculation was all they had, and speculation withered quickly in the rabid, twenty-four-hour news cycle. He had managed to extract himself from the political arena and walk away from the White House without anyone—outside of Black Talon—knowing that he was a treasonous traitor. It was his and Olander's dirty little secret.

They had pulled his Secret Service details a few days ago, which was par for the course. Unlike presidents, who received Secret Service protection for life, vice presidents were only entitled to six months' worth.

He could have extended the protection by paying out of his own pocket, but Black Talon had seized his offshore accounts and frozen most of his assets. He was lucky they had left him this mansion in San Diego. It felt strange to not have armed men trailing him everywhere, but it also felt kind of liberating.

He dove into the large swimming pool out back and felt the California heat vanish as his body sliced through the cool, refreshing water. He stayed under, swimming with smooth, powerful strokes toward the far end of the pool.

When he surfaced, Gabriel Asher stood at the edge with a gun in his hand. He wore dark pants, a loose-fitting white shirt, and mirrored sunglasses.

"Hello, John."

Steinbeck noticed the pistol had a suppressor. Not a good sign. "What the hell are you doing here?" he asked.

Asher's finger had been staged along the frame of the gun, but now slipped inside the trigger guard. "Taking care of unfinished business."

"I did exactly what I was told to do," Steinbeck said as fear flushed through his system. "I resigned and left quietly, just like Olander demanded. Now she ordered you to take me out? Why?"

"Actually..." Asher replied, shifting his grip on the HK45 in his hand. "She doesn't even know I'm here."

"Then you have no right—"

"You helped people target me and Larissa," Asher interjected. "That was a mistake. I have zero tolerance for anyone who tries to harm the woman I love."

"You can't do this!" Steinbeck snarled. "I was the

fucking vice president of the United States, for god's sake!"

"Right," Asher said, and fired a single bullet into his face. *"Was."*

He picked up his spent cartridge and walked away as Steinbeck's body sank to the bottom of the pool in a cloud of crimson.

EPILOGUE

BEHIND ASHER and Larissa's house in the Adirondack Mountains, the bonfire snapped, crackled, and popped in the large stone fire pit. The embers glowed a fiery orange in the twilight as a soft breeze drifted in from the south to whisk away the smoke and mosquitoes.

The house had been repaired, meaning there was no sign of the attack from six months ago. News of former Vice President John Steinbeck's assassination had faded from the news. Olander had asked Asher point-blank if he did it, but he had simply refused to answer. Which, for her, was all the answer she needed. But she never brought it up again.

Rene Perelli continued to cooperate with the government, but Asher had not had any contact with her. Which suited him just fine. He may have found some redemption in her eyes, but he remained unforgiven, and rightfully so.

Congressman Brody Anderson remained part of the Black Talon briefings in order to keep him from causing a media scandal, but he seemed totally cowed by Steinbeck's death. His objections and protests had diminished significantly, and his threats were nowhere to be found. Asher had only crossed paths with the man once, and Anderson had stared at him like he was looking at the grim reaper himself.

Asher swigged from his bottle of beer and turned his head toward the sound of laughter. It was coming from Olander, who stood a short distance away, chatting with Shiomi. Asher allowed himself a little smile. It was rare to hear Olander laugh. He'd been surprised when she accepted the invitation to their campfire get-together. But hell, maybe she was smart enough to realize that she needed to get away from DC sometimes too, to just relax and take a break from the endless grind of the government machine.

Asher looked up, past the mountain peaks, at the shadowy sky above and the stars just starting to show themselves like diamonds scattered across black velvet. He took a deep breath of fresh air and exhaled, long and slow, trying to ease the tension that seemed forever coiled inside him. Being home with Larissa, here in the mountains, always helped.

The others wandered over and took seats around the fire, Chubbs guiding Larissa to her chair and then sitting by her side. The German shepherd glanced over at Asher as if seeking assurance that he had done a good job, and Asher gave him a crooked grin.

After some small talk, Malakai reached over and clasped Shiomi's hand before addressing the group. "So...we have an announcement to make. Just wanted to let everyone know we're thinking about adopting."

Larissa smiled happily. "Oh my god, really? That's great!"

"We're going to start the process anyway," Shiomi said. "Lots of red tape, I'm sure, but it'll be worth it."

"I can help cut through some of that red tape," Olander offered. "Speed up the process a bit for you."

Malakai gave her a little nod. "That'd be great. Appreciate it."

Larissa proposed a toast, and they all drank to the couple. Asher slapped his friend on the shoulder and offered him sincere congratulations. "You'll make a hell of a father."

"Not sure about that. Not like I had a great example growing up." Malakai grinned. "But if I make a mess of it, at least he'll have you as his godfather to steer him straight."

Asher suddenly straightened in his chair. "Godfather? Me?"

"Well, who the hell else would I ask?"

"Guess you got a point there."

After a couple more beers, Asher rose from his chair and walked away from the firelight. As he stood just far enough away from the flames that he couldn't feel their heat, letting the coolness of the summer night wash over his exposed skin, he found himself slipping back into introspection. This was how life should be: good times with great friends. Not blood and death and killing.

Malakai came over and joined him. "Want to be alone?"

"Not necessarily." He could hear Larissa, Shiomi, and Olander all talking together, making all sorts of plans for when the child arrived.

"Still feeling sick of it all?"

"How'd you know?"

"I know *you*," Malakai replied.

"Just a little tired, I guess. This isn't the life I want for Larissa. Hell, for *me*."

They stood in silence, staring into the darkness lit by fireflies, sipping their beers.

Finally, Malakai said, "I feel your pain, but we can't walk away."

"I know," Asher replied. "If it were just you and me, then maybe. But not as long as we have them." He looked over at Larissa and Shiomi.

"I'd rather live my life as an assassin with Shiomi in it than have a peaceful life without her, and I know you feel the same."

"Damn right."

Olander peeled away from the other two women and strolled over to join them. She'd been there for hours, but Asher still felt weird having her at his house. He craved freedom, but she was the one holding the leash.

"Couldn't help but overhear some of what you're saying," she said without preamble. "Getting a bit tired of the fray, boys?"

"You could say that," Asher said. "Spending all my time balls deep in blood doesn't exactly bring me much peace."

"You need a breather?"

"I need out."

Olander shook her head. "I can't do that."

"You mean you *won't* do that."

She shrugged. "Let's not quibble over semantics. Can't, won't...whatever word you choose to use, it means you're not going anywhere. But I am willing to give you a break."

"What kind of break?" Asher didn't even bother to conceal his skepticism.

"Our deal still stands. You want the kill orders to stay lifted, then you work for us, but I'm willing to give you six weeks off to recharge your battery and clear your head."

"Six months."

"Three months. Final offer."

"Better than nothing, I guess."

"Then consider it done," Olander said. "But Gabriel, I need you to come back with your mind right, your head on straight, ready to get back into the game."

"No promises, but I'll see what I can do."

But as soon as he said it, Asher knew it was a lie. He would take the downtime—God knew he and Larissa could use it—but it wouldn't change a damn thing. He wouldn't stop wanting, hoping for, a different life. A *better* life.

Maybe someday, he thought.

The time off wouldn't bring him peace. But maybe, just maybe, it would be enough to keep him in the killing game.

For now, anyway.

A LOOK AT: FURY DIVINE: A LUCAS STONE / PRIMAL JUSTICE NOVEL

BY MARK ALLEN

A HIGH-VOLTAGE ACTION SERIES THAT PROVES SOMETIMES 'THE LAW' AND 'JUSTICE' AREN'T THE SAME THING.

Once a man of war, Lucas Stone becomes the preacher of a small church in Whisper Falls, a mountain town located deep in the rural ruggedness of the northern Adirondacks. As he tries to atone for the sins of his past and find some kind of redemption, he believes the dark days of blood and bullets are behind him.

Turns out, he's dead wrong.

A young girl turns up murdered in the swamp and the local sheriff is too lazy to do much about it, so Stone puts down his Bible, picks up his gun, and starts kicking over rocks to see what comes crawling out. He soon discovers there is a sickening darkness at the heart of Whisper Falls and finds himself with a bullseye on his back.

When the vicious cabal corrupting his new hometown targets the people Stone cares about, he reverts to the cold, hard violence of his warrior days, dispensing primal justice.

Sometimes even a man of God has to rain hell down on sinners...

AVAILABLE NOW.

ABOUT THE AUTHOR

Mark Allen was raised by an ancient clan of ruthless ninjas—though breaking his oath of silence to say so might get him killed. When not practicing shuriken throws or hunting flea markets for a katana, Mark writes high-octane action fiction. He calls it "guns 'n' guts"— packed with twin Micro-Uzis, headshots galore, and punchy prose.

He wrote his first story at 16, won a regional contest soon after, and later published *The Assassin's Prayer*, which sold over 10,000 copies in its first year. Originally optioned by Showtime, the novel blends raw emotion with brutal action, earning Mark a loyal readership.

He lives in the Adirondacks with a skeptical wife, two martial arts–averse daughters, and enough fire-power to keep door-to-door salesmen at bay.